Three Recovery Classics

Hindsfoot Foundation Series
on Spirituality

Three Recovery Classics

As a Man Thinketh
by James Allen

The Greatest Thing in the World
by Henry Drummond

An Instrument of Peace
the St. Francis Prayer

Introduction and commentaries by
Mel B.

iUniverse, Inc.
New York Lincoln Shanghai

Three Recovery Classics
As a Man Thinketh by James Allen
The Greatest Thing in the World by Henry Drummond
An Instrument of Peace the St. Francis Prayer

All Rights Reserved © 2004 by Mel B. (Toledo, Ohio)

No part of this book may be reproduced or transmitted in any form or by any means, graphic, electronic, or mechanical, including photocopying, recording, taping, or by any information storage retrieval system, without the written permission of the publisher.

iUniverse, Inc.

For information address:
iUniverse, Inc.
2021 Pine Lake Road, Suite 100
Lincoln, NE 68512
www.iuniverse.com

ISBN: 0-595-32631-5

Printed in the United States of America

Contents

Introduction *1*
The Gender Thing *3*

Part One

Mel B. on James Allen
How As A Man Thinketh Changed My Life *6*
About James Allen *13*

As a Man Thinketh, by James Allen
Foreword *16*
Thought and Character *17*
Effect of Thought on Circumstances *19*
Effect of Thought on Health and Body *27*
Thought and Purpose *29*
The Thought Factor in Achievement *31*
Visions and Ideals *34*
Serenity *37*

Mel B. on How to Use Allen's Book
Staying the Course in Right Thinking *39*

Part Two

Mel B. on Henry Drummond
Drummond's Great Message on Love *42*
Who Was Henry Drummond? *46*

The Greatest Thing in the World, by Henry Drummond
Paul's Great Message: I Corinthians 13 .... *48*
The Greatest Thing in the World *50*
The Contrast *52*
The Analysis *54*
Patience *56*

Kindness 57
Generosity 59
Humility 60
Courtesy 61
Unselfishness 62
Good Temper 63
Guilelessness and Sincerity 66
Learning and Practicing Love 68
The Defense 71
Knowledge Vanishes Away 72
Everlasting Life 73
The Gospel 75
Knowing God 76
Read it Ninety Times in Ninety Days 77
Be Not Deceived 78

Mel B. on God's Law and God's Love
A Final Comment: Timeless Truth about Law and Love 80

Part Three

Mel B. on The St. Francis Prayer
An Instrument of Peace 84

Notes 89
About the Author 91

Introduction

by Mel B.

It may surprise recovering persons and their friends to find *As A Man Thinketh* and *The Greatest Thing in the World* listed as "recovery classics." I use this term because both books were recommended reading for the early members of Alcoholics Anonymous, especially prior to the Big Book publication. Bill W. and Dr. Bob S., the AA co-founders, had high regard for these publications and passed them on to persons they sought to help.

I found them useful in my own recovery as I struggled from 1950 onward to find new moorings and better principles for living. Both books were offered at modest prices at the AA meetings I attended in the Detroit area. I am confident that the insights I found in them helped both my sobriety and my efforts to get along in the world of work, where I had previously had many problems.

Both books came to us from men schooled in the British Isles. James Allen and Henry Drummond were men of deep faith. They may have seemed different, but each believed in a God of Love who wanted only Good for humankind. Each book offers the individual reader certain principles or guides for spiritual self-improvement at the Soul level.

If you accept the ideas in both books and put them into practice, I believe you'll find beneficial changes coming into your own life. I don't suggest that these changes will be "magical" or "miraculous," although they may seem so for persons who make radical changes in thought. What we ought to be looking for in any self-help book is reasonable growth and understanding.

But are these self-help books? Let's hope they are for readers who are unhappy with their thoughts and feelings and are seeking constructive mood changes.

And what is a *constructive* mood change? Most recovering people need extra help in developing positive outlooks on life, after years of negativity which helped us justify drinking and drugging. The thing to keep in mind always is that in those pursuits we were only seeking our good in the wrong places and with the wrong means. It is a Law of Life that we must choose the right ways and means if we hope to find true happiness and fulfillment.

I cannot improve on the original writings of James Allen or Henry Drummond. But I have added commentary as useful guides for the present age. I urge you to read these recovery classics with an open mind and a feeling of expectancy. You can truly find happiness and serenity as these ideals become part of living clean and sober. I have found them so.

In this collection, I've also included the great Peace Prayer attributed to St. Francis. While Francis himself may not have authored this prayer, it was a favorite meditation for AA cofounder Bill W. and is certainly a "recovery classic."

Mel B.
Toledo, Ohio
July 12, 2004

The Gender Thing

by Mel B.

As customary in their times, both James Allen and Henry Drummond used "man" and male pronouns to represent either sex. Were they writing today, their constructions would reflect the current gender-free styles—though this is still awkward for singular references.

In this book, we have reproduced both authors' writings as they delivered them at the times. We hope that our readers will accept this in good humor and will know that we have no wish to make any statement either against or for current trends in writing. Our purpose here is to offer ideas and principles that will serve readers well in their personal lives. Our focus is on recovery, and we believe that both men and women must follow the same recovery principles if they hope to find sobriety and happiness.

Should some readers feel that *As A Man Thinketh* uses too many masculine pronouns, we urge them to get a copy that has been titled *As A Woman Thinketh*. It is exactly the same book, except for a complete gender change! And if you want gender identification almost completely eliminated, check your bookstores for copies of *As I Think* and *As You Think*. Both books represent Allen's original ideas but have been adapted for present-day readers.

Again, our sole purpose here is to offer classic books that can be highly useful to people in recovery.

Part One
James Allen

How *As A Man Thinketh* Changed My Life

by Mel B.

In 1951, I was completing my first year of sobriety in Alcoholics Anonymous. At age 25, I was then looked upon as one of the "very young" whose chances of remaining continuously sober were viewed skeptically by older AA members. There was good reason for this view; numerous young people seemed to be shuttling in and out of the program, as they still do today. But one significant change has been the lowering of age levels. We are now accustomed to seeing many teenagers in AA as well as a large number of younger people who use other drugs along with alcohol.

I know today that my emotional state was very precarious, but the saving quality was a strong inner determination to find and maintain sobriety at all costs and in the face of any obstacle. My drinking history had covered only ten years—from a first experiment with wine at about age 14 to an acceptance of the AA program at age 24. But those ten years had been a time of very destructive drinking leading to complete helplessness and dependency. In my alcoholism, I had been a prisoner of King Alcohol, and I wanted to end this imprisonment and stay free.

But true freedom comes at a price for alcoholics and other addicts. Putting the plug in the jug, as we say in AA, is the most important move alcoholics can make. But unless you're unusual, you may then find yourself facing long days of endless boredom, fierce depression, and complete frustration. There are regrets about the past and fears for the future, though AA promises that these should end. There may be difficulty in meeting responsibilities, finding the right work, and in getting along with ourselves and other personalities who are just as troublesome!

At the back of everything, however, is the way we think, feel, and act. Most of us still avoid the responsibility of looking at our own role in creating our own suffering and problems. It is always easier to blame others—to shift the burden to our parents or to an uncaring and heartless "society." It is not difficult to find justification for this, because parents have often been unable or unwilling to meet most of our primary needs and society has always seemed woefully lacking and inadequate. It is also easy to blame the more successful members of society for its general failings.

James Allen, in his remarkable little book, would have none of this. He placed the *entire* responsibility on the individual, apparently without exception. Using a line captured from Proverbs 23:7 ("As he thinketh in his heart, so is he") he described what is sometimes called the Law of Being, or the Great Law. We are what we think, and if we would change our lives, we must change our thoughts.

What does this have to do with recovering alcoholics who are striving to follow the AA program? It meshes with it perfectly, for the most basic idea in AA is that alcoholics have created their own condition and are also responsible for their own recoveries. *Alcoholics Anonymous,* the basic text of AA, makes this point repeatedly. "Selfishness—self-centeredness! That, we think, is the root of our troubles," it states. "Driven by a hundred forms of fear, self-delusion, self-seeking, and self-pity, we step on the toes of our fellows and they retaliate. Sometimes they hurt us, seemingly without provocation, but we invariably find that at some time in the past we have made decisions based on self which later placed us in a position to be hurt."

"So our troubles, we think, are basically of our own making," it goes on to explain. "They arise out of ourselves, and the alcoholic is an extreme example of self-will run riot, though he usually doesn't think so. Above everything, we alcoholics must be rid of this selfishness. We must, or it kills us!"[1]

Alcoholics do try to avoid all the implications of such statements, particularly when it comes to sober living. It is easy to admit that one has been responsible for the single, willful act of picking up a drink, but many people will balk at accepting responsibility for *everything* in their lives. After all, we can easily ask, are we responsible for the wars, crime, illnesses, economic disasters, accidents, and other fates which befall us? Where do we draw the line between *individual* responsibility and social conditions which seem to be beyond our reach?

It would be naïve and simplistic to say that Allen has a complete answer to such questions in a book that can be read in less than an hour. But as a long-time member of AA, I can say with certainty that most alcoholics, even in recovery, fall far short of taking full responsibility for their life conditions. Even in sobriety, the business of blaming can go on, and we sometimes indulge it by supposing that we are being compassionate by listening to a self-piteous person describe the indignities he is suffering at the hands of a mean boss or a spiteful ex-spouse. The problem with this misplaced compassion is that by allowing some to get away with blaming others for their conditions, we also make it possible to do the same thing ourselves. And this means that we are not likely to get at the roots of our general troubles with the same honesty and soul-searching that we applied to understanding our alcoholism.

But there are right ways and wrong ways to present this concept of individual responsibility. When we see people in terribly wretched conditions, we only pour more salt on their wounds if we tell them they created those conditions. I like to think that the proper way to deal with very troubled people is the Salvation Army way. Salvationists, ever since their founding in 1865, have always given help to alcoholics and others whose conditions appear to be self-imposed. While preaching may accompany this, it is never done in a self-righteous manner or in a way that implies condemnation. There is always the assurance that things can or may be different in the future, that "a person may be down, but is never out." The message should always be that as human beings we are prone to error but through the Grace of God our lives can change. But we can become aware of this Grace only as individuals; this is the Free Will all of us have. Anything that is forced on us against our will cannot do its redeeming work.

As recovering people in Twelve Step programs, we can resort to Allen's timeless message by taking it in each of the seven segments he offers. They can be applied and studied as we feel the need. Here is a suggested way to relate them to everyday concerns of modern life and recovery:

Thought and Character

Twelve Step programs continuously address issues of character defects or shortcomings on the path to character building. Few people quarrel with the belief that character problems go hand-in-hand with addictions. But why do we have them and what can we do about them? According to Allen, we created our present character and also have the power to change it for the better. And how do we do this? By choosing the type of thoughts we will habitually entertain. "A noble and Godlike character is not a thing of favor or chance," he writes, "but is the natural result of continued effort in right thinking, the effect of long-cherished association with Godlike thoughts. An ignoble and bestial character, by the same process, is the result of the continued harboring of groveling thoughts."

There it is, for every recovering person to ponder. Again and again, we are warned about the risks and dangers of holding resentments and other bad feelings. But have we really understood the harm we do to ourselves in the process? And do we really believe that the payoff for long effort in good thinking is a transformed character? There need not be any argument about the truth of Allen's statements. Individuals can easily test them out in their own lives, using the Twelve Steps as a guide to action.

Effect of Thought on Circumstances

This is the longest of Allen's segments and it should be studied persistently until it becomes embedded in one's heart of hearts. Most of us would like to improve our circumstances in one way or another. A few complain that the AA program gives them sobriety, but little else changes: the job is still boring, creditors are unrelenting in their demands, a hoped-for promotion never materialized, and mistakes from the past still have the power to haunt us today. And while we would like to change our circumstances, there are numerous barriers to improvement: insufficient education or training, a poor work record, a roller-coaster economy, or prejudice on the part of others. We seem to be trapped or stuck right where we are.

But according to Allen, the way out is to change one's thinking. "That circumstances *grow* out of thought every man knows who has for any length of time practiced self-control and self-purification," Allen says, "for he will have noticed that the alteration in his circumstances has been in exact ratio with his altered mental condition. So true is this that when a man earnestly applies himself to remedy the defects in his character, and makes swift and marked progress, he passes rapidly through a succession of vicissitudes."

Here again, the proof is in the practice. Make a determined and persistent effort to reverse a negative pattern of thought and see for yourself the changes in your life. They may be slight at first, or even accompanied by what appear to be disappointments or setbacks, but the progress over time should be clear and continuous. This has happened often in Twelve Step experience, and we can use these examples as inspirations for ourselves. Study Allen's words carefully, and apply them to your own view of your current circumstances. And remember the rule, or law, he gives as both a warning and a promise: "A particular train of thought persisted in, be it good or bad, cannot fail to produce its results on the character and circumstances. A man cannot *directly* choose his circumstances, but he can choose his thoughts, and so indirectly, yet surely, shape his circumstance."

Effect of Thought on Health and the Body

Twelve Step programs focus on addictions and mental health rather than physical well-being. But in Allen's lifetime, a number of people were laying the groundwork for what is now widely accepted in the medical profession: that the mind and the emotions influence bodily health. Allen described the body as being "the servant of the mind" and also said that if you would perfect and renew your body, guard and beautify your mind. I think the experience of AA would tend to prove him right. Apart from the physical ills that come from compulsive drinking, there is also some physical destruction from the resentments and other savage emotions that are present in active alcoholism. There can be noticeable improvements in physical health when people become clean and sober by following a good program.

Thought and Purpose

One of AA's greatest strengths is its emphasis on staying sober at all costs. No excuse ever suffices to justify drinking for the alcoholic. And at every AA meeting, it's stated that AA's primary purpose is to help the alcoholic who still suffers. The underlying truth is that there can be no real success without purpose. As Allen says, "Until thought is linked with purpose there can be no intelligent accomplishment." This is a warning against the indecision and drifting that keep many from finding sobriety. It's also a reminder that reaching other goals also requires a linkage of thought and purpose.

The Thought Factor in Achievement

Why do some persons find sobriety and happiness in Twelve Step programs while others stumble and fall? Is it a matter of luck or of God blessing one person while hiding His face from others?

According to Allen, it's all a matter of law, and people reap the harvest of their own thoughts. "All that a man achieves and all that he fails to achieve is the direct result of his own thoughts," Allen writes. "In a justly ordered universe, where loss of equipoise would mean total destruction, individual responsibility must be absolute." He also has something to say about the willingness that's required if a person wishes to acquire the strength he sees in another. This relates perfectly to a slogan often expressed in AA: "Willingness is the key."

Visions and Ideals

Though visionaries and dreamers are sometimes scorned in the "practical" world, they are really the architects of human progress. Allen even calls dreamers "the saviors of the world." He insists that your dreams and ideals have the power to take you out of any uncongenial environment, if you but remain true to them. You cannot grow within and stand still without. Twelve Step devotees who read this segment should also reread the chapter, "A Vision for You," in the AA Big Book. Back in 1939, the AA pioneers wrote: "Our hope is that when this chip of a book is launched on the world tide of alcoholism, defeated drinkers will seize upon it, to follow its suggestion.... They will approach still other sick ones and Fellowships of Alcoholics Anonymous may spring up in every city and hamlet, havens for those who must find a way out." At the time this was written, AA had about one hundred members, some of them still shaky, and the book was published largely on credit. As the twenty-first century dawned, AA membership stood at about two million worldwide, and nearly 20 million copies of the "chip of a book" had been published. Talk about the power of a vision!

Serenity

It should surprise AA members to find Allen using "Serenity" as the title of his final segment. He calls it "calmness of mind" and believes it to be one of the "beautiful jewels of wisdom." This was long before AA was formed and found its way to the now world-famous Serenity Prayer. Allen writes: "That exquisite poise of character which we call serenity is the last lesson of culture; it is the flowering of life, the fruit of the soul. It is precious as wisdom, more to be desired than gold—yea, than even fine gold. How insignificant mere moneymaking looks in comparison with a serene life—a life that dwells in the ocean of Truth, beneath the waves, beyond the reach of Tempests, in the Eternal Calm."

A Wonderful Book for People in Recovery

The last thing I can say about *As A Man Thinketh* is to describe it as a wonderful book for people in recovery. In seven easy-to-read segments, it defines for us the Great Law under which we all live, and which Jesus actually alluded to in the Sermon on the Mount. We reap what we sow, we are what we think, we must clean the inside of the cup to have a good outer life. This is also the way of the Twelve Step program, and Allen's book will help any person who truly applies its essential ideas in his/her life.

And by the way, there are small, compact versions of the book around which can be handy for use throughout the day. I urge you to find one and to consult it during waiting periods and other intervals. If you follow the suggested principles, it can change your life for the better and it will also enhance your sobriety.

About James Allen

by Mel B.

A number of James Allen's books are still published, but none ever approached the popularity of *As A Man Thinketh*. Though written nearly one hundred years ago, it is still offered in several editions and has never lost its power to change lives. It was a forerunner of many contemporary self-help books emphasizing the importance of thought and feeling.

James Allen was born in Leicester, England, in 1864. Family poverty and the untimely death of his father forced him to leave school and work in a clerical capacity. This may have brought his writing talent to light, though he never made more than a bare living as a writer. Nonetheless, he did move with his family to Ilfracombe on England's west coast to pursue a full-time career as a writer.

As A Man Thinketh was said to be the second of Allen's nineteen books, and was already in its fourth edition by 1908. It has never been out of print, and historian Charles Braden reported that by 1960 eight editions were available from publishers. It has since been revised in gender-neutral editions and Hallmark has produced an unusually elegant version with copy enhancements. (The version used here retains the original writing.)

Allen died in 1912, leaving little information for biographers. Though he died poor, *As A Man Thinketh* has been a legacy beyond measure.

As a Man Thinketh

by James Allen

First published c. 1908

Foreword

This little volume (the result of meditation and experience) is not intended as an exhaustive treatise on the much-written-upon subject of the power of thought. It is suggestive rather than explanatory, its object being to stimulate men and women to the discovery and perception of the truth that—

"They themselves are makers of themselves"

by virtue of the thoughts which they choose and encourage; that mind is the master weaver, both of the inner garment of character and the outer garment of circumstance, and that, as they may have hitherto woven in ignorance and pain they may now weave in enlightenment and happiness.

James Allen
Ilfracombe, England
Circa 1908

Thought and Character

The aphorism, "As a man thinketh in his heart so is he," not only embraces the whole of a man's being, but is so comprehensive as to reach out to every condition and circumstance of his life. A man is literally *what he thinks*, his character being the complete sum of all his thoughts.

As the plant springs from, and could not be without, the seed, so every act of a man springs from the hidden seeds of thought, and could not have appeared without them. This applies equally to those acts called "spontaneous" and "unpremeditated" as to those which are deliberately executed.

Act is the blossom of thought, and joy and suffering are its fruits; thus does a man garner in the sweet and bitter fruitage of his own husbandry.

> Thought in the mind hath made us. What we are
> By thought was wrought and built. If a man's mind
> Hath evil thoughts, pain comes on him as comes
> The wheel the ox behind.... If one endure in purity
> Of thought, joy follows him as his own shadow—sure.

Man is a growth by law, and not a creation by artifice, and cause and effect is as absolute and undeviating in the hidden realm of thought as in the world of visible and material things. A noble and Godlike character is not a thing of favor or chance, but is the natural result of continued effort in right thinking, the effect of long-cherished association with Godlike thoughts. An ignoble and bestial character, by the same process, is the result of the continued harboring of groveling thoughts.

Man is made or unmade by himself; in the armory of thought he forges the weapons by which he destroys himself; he also fashions the tools with which he builds for himself heavenly mansions of joy and strength and peace. By the right choice and true application of thought, man ascends to the Divine Perfection; by the abuse and wrong application of thought, he descends below the level of the beast. Between these two extremes are all the grades of character, and man is their maker and master.

Of all the beautiful truths pertaining to the soul which have been restored and brought to light in this age, none is more gladdening or fruitful of divine promise and confidence than this—that man is the master of thought, the molder of character, and the maker and shaper of condition, environment, and destiny.

As a being of Power, Intelligence, and Love, and the lord of his own thoughts, man holds the key to every situation, and contains within himself that transforming and regenerative agency by which he may make himself what he wills.

Man is always the master, even in his weakest and most abandoned state; but in his weakness and degradation he is the foolish master who misgoverns his "household." When he begins to reflect upon his condition, and to search diligently for the Law upon which his being is established, he then becomes the wise master, directing his energies with intelligence, and fashioning his thoughts to fruitful issues. Such is the *conscious* master, and man can only thus become by discovering *within himself* the laws of thought; which discovery is totally a matter of application, self-analysis, and experience.

Only by much searching and mining are gold and diamonds obtained, and man can find every truth connected with his being if he will dig deep into the mine of his soul; and that he is the maker of his character, the molder of his life, and the builder of his destiny, he may unerringly prove, if he will watch, control, and alter his thoughts, tracing their effects upon himself, upon others, and upon his life and circumstances, linking cause and effect by patient practice and investigation, and utilizing his every experience, even to the most trivial, everyday occurrence, as a means of obtaining that knowledge of himself which is Understanding, Wisdom, Power. In this direction, as in no other, is the law absolute that "He that seeketh findeth; and to him that knocketh it shall be opened"; for only by patience, practice, and ceaseless importunity can a man enter the Door of the Temple of Knowledge.

Effect of Thought on Circumstances

A man's mind may be likened to a garden, which may be intelligently cultivated or allowed to run wild; but whether cultivated or neglected, it must, and will, *bring forth*. If no useful seeds are *put* into it, then an abundance of useless weed-seeds will *fall* therein, and will continue to produce their kind.

Just as a gardener cultivates his plot, keeping it free from weeds, and growing the flowers and fruits which he requires, so may a man tend the garden of his mind, weeding out all the wrong, useless, and impure thoughts, and cultivating toward perfection the flowers and fruits of right, useful, and pure thoughts. By pursuing this process, a man sooner or later discovers that he is the master-gardener of his soul, the director of his life. He also reveals, within himself, the laws of thought, and understands, with ever-increasing accuracy, how the thought-forces and mind-elements operate in the shaping of his character, circumstances, and destiny.

Thought and character are one, and as character can only manifest and discover itself through environment and circumstance, the outer conditions of a person's life will always be found to be harmoniously related to his inner state. This does not mean that a man's circumstances at any given time are an indication of his *entire* character, but that those circumstances are so intimately connected with some vital thought-element within himself that, for the time being, they are indispensable to his development.

Every man is where he is by the law of his being; the thoughts which he has built into his character have brought him there, and in the arrangement of his life there is no element of chance, but all is the result of a law which cannot err. This is just as true of those who feel "out of harmony" with their surroundings as of those who are contented with them.

As a progressive and evolving being, man is where he is that he may learn that he may grow; and as he learns the spiritual lesson which any circumstance contains for him, it passes away and gives place to other circumstances.

Man is buffeted by circumstances so long as he believes himself to be the creature of outside conditions, but when he realizes that he is a creative power, and that he may command the hidden soil and seeds of his being out of which circumstances grow, he then becomes the rightful master of himself.

That circumstances *grow* out of thought every man knows who has for any length of time practiced self-control and self-purification, for he will have noticed that the alteration in his circumstances has been in exact ratio with his altered mental condition. So true is this that when a man earnestly applies himself to remedy the defects in his character, and makes swift and marked progress, he passes rapidly through a succession of vicissitudes.

The soul attracts that which it secretly harbors; that which it loves, and also that which it fears; it reaches the height of its cherished aspirations; it falls to the level of its unchastened desires—and circumstances are the means by which the soul receives its own.

Every thought-seed sown or allowed to fall into the mind, and to take root there, produces its own, blossoming sooner or later into act, and bearing its own fruitage of opportunity and circumstance. Good thoughts bear good fruit, bad thoughts bad fruit.

The outer world of circumstance shapes itself to the inner world of thought, and both pleasant and unpleasant external conditions are factors which make for the ultimate good of the individual. As the reaper of his own harvest, man learns both by suffering and bliss.

Following the inmost desires, aspirations, thoughts, by which he allows himself to be dominated (pursuing the will-o'-the-wisps of impure imaginings or steadfastly walking the highway of strong and high endeavor), a man at last arrives at their fruition and fulfillment in the outer conditions of his life. The laws of growth and adjustment everywhere obtain.

A man does not come to the almshouse or the jail by the tyranny of fate or circumstance, but by the pathway of groveling thoughts and base desires. Nor does a pure-minded man fall suddenly into crime by stress of any mere external force; the criminal thought had long been secretly fostered in the heart, and the hour of opportunity revealed its gathered power. Circumstance does not make the man; it reveals him to himself. No such conditions can exist as descending into vice and its attendant sufferings apart from vicious inclinations, or ascending into virtue and its pure happiness without the continued cultivation of virtuous aspirations; and man, therefore, as the Lord and master of thought, is the maker of himself, the shaper and author of environment. Even at birth the soul comes to its own, and through every step of its earthly pilgrimage it attracts those combinations of conditions which reveal itself, which are the reflections of its own purity and impurity, its strength and weakness.

Men do not attract that which they *want,* but that which they *are.* Their whims, fancies, and ambitions are thwarted at every step, but their inmost thoughts and desires are fed with their own food, be it foul or clean. The "divinity that shapes our ends" is in ourselves; it is our very self. Man is manacled only by himself; thought and action are the jailers of Fate—they imprison, being base; they are also the angels of Freedom—they liberate, being noble. Not what he wishes and prays for does a man get, but what he justly earns. His wishes and prayers are only gratified and answered when they harmonize with his thoughts and actions.

In the light of this truth, what, then, is the meaning of "fighting against circumstances"? It means that a man is continually revolting against an *effect* without, while all the time he is nourishing and preserving its *cause* in his heart. That cause may take the form of a conscious vice or an unconscious weakness; but whatever it is, it stubbornly retards the efforts of its possessor, and thus calls aloud for remedy.

Men are anxious to improve their circumstances, but are unwilling to improve themselves; they therefore remain bound. The man who does not shrink from self-crucifixion can never fail to accomplish the object upon which his heart is set. This is as true of earthly as of heavenly things. Even the man whose sole object is to acquire wealth must be prepared to make great personal sacrifices before he can accomplish his object; and how much more so he who would realize a strong and well-poised life?

Here is a man who is wretchedly poor. He is extremely anxious that his surroundings and home comforts should be improved. Yet all the time he shirks his work, and considers he is justified in trying to deceive his employer on the ground of the insufficiency of his wages. Such a man does not understand the simplest rudiments of those principles which are the basis of true prosperity, and is not only totally unfitted to rise out of his wretchedness, but is actually attracting to himself a still deeper wretchedness by dwelling in, and acting out, indolent, deceptive, and unmanly thoughts.

Here is a rich man who is the victim of a painful and persistent disease as the result of gluttony. He is willing to give large sums of money to get rid of it, but he will not sacrifice his gluttonous desires. He wants to gratify his taste for rich and unnatural foods and have his health as well. Such a man is totally unfit to have health, because he has not yet learned the first principles of a healthy life.

Here is an employer of labor who adopts crooked measures to avoid paying the regulation wage, and, in the hope of making larger profits, reduces the wages of his work-people. Such a man is altogether unfitted for prosperity, and when he finds himself bankrupt, both as regards reputation and riches, he blames circumstances, not knowing that he is the sole author of his condition.

I have introduced these three cases merely as illustrative of the truth that man is the causer (though nearly always unconsciously) of his circumstances, and that, while aiming at a good end, he is continually frustrating its accomplishment by encouraging thoughts and desires which cannot possibly harmonize with that end. Such cases could be multiplied and varied almost indefinitely, but this is not necessary, as the reader can, if he so resolves, trace the action of the laws of thought in his own mind and life, and until this is done, mere external facts cannot serve as a ground of reasoning.

Circumstances, however, are so complicated, thought is so deeply rooted, and the conditions of happiness vary so vastly with individuals, that a man's *entire* soul condition (although it may be known to himself) cannot be judged by another from the external aspect of his life alone. A man may be honest in certain directions, yet suffer privations; a man may be dishonest in certain directions, yet acquire wealth; but the conclusion usually formed that the one man fails *because of his particular honesty*, and that the other prospers *because of his particular dishonesty*, is the result of a superficial judgment, which assumes that the dishonest man is almost totally corrupt, and the honest man almost entirely virtuous. In the light of a deeper knowledge and wider experience, such judgment is found to be erroneous. The dishonest man may have some admirable virtues which the other does not possess; and the honest man obnoxious vices which are absent in the other. The honest man reaps the good results of his honest thoughts and acts; he also brings upon himself the sufferings which his vices produce. The dishonest man likewise garners his own suffering and happiness.

It is pleasing to human vanity to believe that one suffers because of one's virtue; but not until a man has extirpated every sickly, bitter, and impure thought from his mind, and washed every sinful stain from his soul, can he be in a position to know and declare that his sufferings are the result of his good, and not of his bad qualities; and on the way to, yet long before he has reached, that supreme perfection, he will have found, working in his mind and life, the Great Law which is absolutely just, and which cannot, therefore, give good for evil, evil for good. Possessed of such knowledge, he will then know, looking back upon his past ignorance and blindness, that his life is, and always was, justly ordered, and that all his past experiences, good and bad, were the equitable outworking of his evolving, yet unevolved self.

Good thoughts and actions can never produce bad results; bad thoughts and actions can never produce good results. This is but saying that nothing can come from corn but corn, nothing from nettles but nettles. Men understand this law in the natural world, and work with it; but few understand it in the mental and moral world (though its operation there is just as simple and undeviating), and they, therefore, do not cooperate with it.

Suffering is *always* the effect of wrong thought in some direction. It is an indication that the individual is out of harmony with himself, with the Law of his being. The sole and supreme use of suffering is to purify, to burn out all that is useless and impure. Suffering ceases for him who is pure. There could be no object in burning gold after the dross had been removed, and a perfectly pure and enlightened being could not suffer.

The circumstances which a man encounters with suffering are the result of his own mental inharmony. The circumstances which a man encounters with blessedness are the result of his own mental harmony. Blessedness, not material possessions, is the measure of right thought; wretchedness, not lack of material possessions, is the measure of wrong thought. A man may be cursed and rich; he may be blessed and poor. Blessedness and riches are only joined together when the riches are rightly and wisely used;

and the poor man only descends into wretchedness when he regards his lot as a burden unjustly imposed.

Indigence and indulgence are the two extremes of wretchedness. They are both equally unnatural and the result of mental disorder. A man is not rightly conditioned until he is a happy, healthy, and prosperous being; and happiness, health, and prosperity are the result of a harmonious adjustment of the inner with the outer, of the man with his surroundings.

A man only begins to be a man when he ceases to whine and revile, and commences to search for the hidden justice which regulates his life. And as he adapts his mind to that regulating factor, he ceases to accuse others as the cause of his condition, and builds himself up in strong and noble thoughts; ceases to kick against circumstances, but begins to *use* them as aids to his more rapid progress, and as a means of discovering the hidden powers and possibilities within himself.

Law, not confusion, is the dominating principle in the universe; justice, not injustice, is the soul and substance of life; and righteousness, not corruption, is the molding and moving force in the spiritual government of the world. This being so, man has but to right himself to find that the universe is right; and during the process of putting himself right, he will find that as he alters his thoughts towards things and other people, things and other people will alter toward him.

The proof of this truth is in every person, and it therefore admits of easy investigation by systematic introspection and self-analysis. Let a man radically alter his thoughts, and he will be astonished at the rapid transformation it will effect in the material conditions of his life.

Men imagine that thought can be kept secret, but it cannot; it rapidly crystallizes into habit, and habit solidifies into circumstance. Bestial thoughts crystallize into habits of drunkenness and sensuality, which solidify into circumstances of destitution and disease; impure thoughts of every kind crystallize into enervating and confusing habits, which solidify into distracting and adverse circumstances; thoughts of fear, doubt, and indecision crystallize into weak, unmanly, and irresolute habits, which solidify into circumstances of failure, indigence, and slavish dependence. Lazy thoughts crystallize into habits of uncleanliness and dishonesty, which solidify into circumstances of foulness and beggary; hateful and condemnatory thoughts crystallize into habits of accusation and violence, which solidify into circumstances of injury and persecution; and selfish thoughts of all kinds crystallize into habits of self-seeking, which solidify into circumstances more or less distressing.

On the other hand, beautiful thoughts of all kinds crystallize into habits of grace and kindliness, which solidify into genial and sunny circumstances; pure thoughts crystallize into habits of temperance and self-control, which solidify into circumstances of repose and peace; thoughts of courage, self-reliance, and decision crystallize into manly habits, which solidify into circumstances of success, plenty, and freedom.

Energetic thoughts crystallize into habits of cleanliness and industry, which solidify into circumstances of pleasantness; gentle and forgiving thoughts crystallize into habits of gentleness, which solidify into protective and preservative circumstances; loving and unselfish thoughts crystallize into habits of self-forgetfulness for others, which solidify into circumstances of sure and abiding prosperity and true riches.

A particular train of thought persisted in, be it good or bad, cannot fail to produce its results on the character and circumstances. A man cannot *directly* choose his circumstances, but he can choose his thoughts, and so indirectly, yet surely, shape his circumstances.

Nature helps every man to the gratification of the thoughts which he most encourages, and opportunities are presented which will most speedily bring to the surface both the good and evil thoughts.

Let a man cease from his sinful thoughts, and all the world will soften toward him, and be ready to help him; let him put away his weakly and sickly thoughts, and lo! opportunities will spring up on every hand to aid his strong resolves; let him encourage good thoughts, and no hard fate shall bind him down to wretchedness and shame. The world is your kaleidoscope, and the varying combinations of colors which at every succeeding moment it presents to you are the exquisitely adjusted pictures of your ever-moving thoughts.

You will be what you will to be;
Let failure find its false content
In that poor word, "environment,"
But spirit scorns it, and is free.

It masters time, it conquers space;
It cows that boastful trickster, Chance,
And bids the tyrant Circumstance
Uncrown, and fill a servant's place.

The human Will, that force unseen,
The offspring of a deathless Soul,
Can hew a way to any goal,
Though walls of granite intervene.

Be not impatient in delay,
But wait as one who understands;
When spirit rises and commands,
The gods are ready to obey.

Effect of Thought on Health and Body

The body is the servant of the mind. It obeys the operations of the mind, whether they be deliberately chosen or automatically expressed. At the bidding of unlawful thoughts the body sinks rapidly into disease and decay; at the command of glad and beautiful thoughts it becomes clothed with youthfulness and beauty.

Disease and health, like circumstances, are rooted in thought. Sickly thoughts will express themselves through a sickly body. Thoughts of fear have been known to kill a man as speedily as a bullet, and they are continually killing thousands of people just as surely though less rapidly. The people who live in fear of disease are the people who get it. Anxiety quickly demoralizes the whole body, and lays it open to the entrance of disease; while impure thoughts, even if not physically indulged, will soon shatter the nervous system.

Strong, pure, and happy thoughts build up the body in vigor and grace. The body is a delicate and plastic instrument, which responds readily to the thoughts by which it is impressed, and habits of thought will produce their own effects, good or bad, upon it.

Men will continue to have impure and poisoned blood so long as they propagate unclean thoughts. Out of a clean heart comes a clean life and a clean body. Out of a defiled mind proceeds a defiled life and corrupt body. Thought is the fountain of action, life and manifestation; make the fountain pure, and all will be pure.

Change of diet will not help a man who will not change his thoughts. When a man makes his thoughts pure, he no longer desires impure food.

Clean thoughts make clean habits. The so-called saint who does not wash his body is not a saint. He who has strengthened and purified his thoughts does not need to consider the malevolent microbe.

If you would perfect your body, guard your mind. If you would renew your body, beautify your mind. Thoughts of malice, envy, disappointment, despondency, rob the body of its health and grace. A sour face does not come by chance; it is made by sour thoughts. Wrinkles that mar are drawn by folly, passion, pride.

I know a woman of ninety-six who has the bright, innocent face of a girl. I know a man well under middle age whose face is drawn into inharmonious contours. The one is the result of a sweet and sunny disposition; the other is the outcome of passion and discontent.

As you cannot have a sweet and wholesome abode unless you admit the air and sunshine freely into your rooms, so a strong body and a bright, happy, or serene countenance can only result from the free admittance into the mind of thoughts of joy and goodwill and serenity.

On the faces of the aged there are wrinkles made by sympathy, others by strong and pure thought, others are carved by passion. Who cannot distinguish them? With those who have lived righteously, age is calm, peaceful, and softly mellowed, like the setting sun. I have recently seen a philosopher on his deathbed. He was not old except in years. He died as sweetly and peacefully as he had lived.

There is no physician like cheerful thought for dissipating the ills of the body; there is no comforter to compare with goodwill for dispersing the shadows of grief and sorrow. To live continually in thoughts of ill will, cynicism, suspicion, and envy, is to be confined in a self-made prison hole. But to think well of all, to be cheerful with all, to patiently learn to find the good in all—such unselfish thoughts are the very portals of heaven; and to dwell day by day in thoughts of peace toward every creature will bring abounding peace to their possessor.

Thought and Purpose

Until thought is linked with purpose there is no intelligent accomplishment. With the majority the bark of thought is allowed to "drift" upon the ocean of life. Aimlessness is a vice, and such drifting must not continue for him who would steer clear of catastrophe and destruction.

They who have no central purpose in their life fall an easy prey to petty worries, fears, troubles, and self-pityings, all of which are indications of weakness, which lead, just as surely as deliberately planned sins (though by a different route), to failure, unhappiness, and loss, for weakness cannot persist in a power-evolving universe.

A man should conceive of a legitimate purpose in his heart, and set out to accomplish it. He should make this purpose the centralizing point of his thoughts. It may take the form of a spiritual ideal, or it may be a worldly object, according to his nature at the time being. But whichever it is, he should steadily focus his thought-forces upon the object which he has set before him. He should make this purpose his supreme duty, and should devote himself to its attainment, not allowing his thoughts to wander away into ephemeral fancies, longings, and imaginings. This is the royal road to self-control and true concentration of thought. Even if he fails again and again to accomplish his purpose (as he necessarily must until weakness is overcome), the *strength of character* gained will be the measure of his *true* success, and this will form a new starting-point for future power and triumph.

Those who are not prepared for the apprehension of a *great* purpose, should fix the thoughts upon the faultless performance of their duty, no matter how insignificant their task may appear. Only in this way can the thoughts be gathered and focused, and resolution and energy be developed, which being done, there is nothing which may not be accomplished.

The weakest soul, knowing its own weakness, and believing this truth—*that strength can only be developed by effort and practice*—will, thus believing, at once begin to exert itself, and adding effort to effort, patience to patience, and strength to strength, will never cease to develop, and will at last grow divinely strong.

As the physically weak man can make himself strong by careful and patient training, so the man of weak thoughts can make them strong by exercising himself in right thinking.

To put away aimlessness and weakness, and to begin to think with purpose, is to enter the ranks of those strong ones who only recognize failure as one of the pathways to attainment; who make all conditions serve them, and who think strongly, attempt fearlessly, and accomplish masterfully.

Having conceived of his purpose, a man should mentally mark out a *straight* pathway to its achievement, looking neither to the right nor to the left. Doubts and fears should be rigorously excluded; they are disintegrating elements which break up the straight line of effort, rendering it crooked, ineffectual, useless. Thoughts of doubt and fear never accomplish anything, and never can. They always lead to failure. Purpose, energy, power to do, and all strong thoughts cease when doubt and fear creep in.

The will to do springs from the knowledge that we *can* do. Doubt and fear are the great enemies of knowledge, and he who encourages them, who does not slay them, thwarts himself at every step.

He who has conquered doubt and fear has conquered failure. His every thought is allied with power, and all difficulties are bravely met and wisely overcome. His purposes are seasonably planted, and they bloom and bring forth fruit which does not fall prematurely to the ground.

Thought allied fearlessly to purpose becomes creative force. He who *knows* this is ready to become something higher and stronger than a mere bundle of wavering thoughts and fluctuating sensations. He who *does* this has become the conscious and intelligent wielder of his mental powers.

The Thought Factor in Achievement

All that a man achieves and all that he fails to achieve is the direct result of his own thoughts. In a justly ordered universe, where loss of equipoise would mean total destruction, individual responsibility must be absolute. A man's weakness and strength, purity and impurity, are his own, and not another man's. They are brought about by himself, and not by another; and they can only be altered by himself, never by another. His condition is also his own, and not another man's. His suffering and his happiness are evolved from within. As he thinks, so he is; as he continues to think, so he remains.

A strong man cannot help a weaker unless that weaker is *willing* to be helped, and even then the weak man must become strong of himself. He must, by his own efforts, develop the strength which he admires in another. None but himself can alter his condition.

It has been usual for men to think and to say, "Many men are slaves because one is an oppressor; let us hate the oppressor." Now, however, there is among an increasing few a tendency to reverse this judgment, and to say, "One man is an oppressor because many are slaves; let us despise the slaves." The truth is that oppressor and slave are cooperators in ignorance, and, while seeming to afflict each other, are in reality afflicting themselves. A perfect Knowledge perceives the action of law in the weakness of the oppressed and the misapplied power of the oppressor. A perfect Love, seeing the suffering which both states entail, condemns neither. A perfect Compassion embraces both oppressor and oppressed.

He who has conquered weakness, and has put away all selfish thoughts, belongs neither to oppressor nor oppressed. He is free.

A man can only rise, conquer, and achieve by lifting up his thoughts. He can only remain weak, and abject, and miserable by refusing to lift up his thoughts.

Before a man can achieve anything, even in worldly things, he must lift his thoughts above slavish animal indulgence. He may not, in order to succeed, give up *all* animality and selfishness, by any means; but a portion of it must, at least, be sacrificed. A man whose first thought is bestial indulgence could neither think clearly nor plan methodically. He could not find and develop his latent resources, and would fail in any undertaking. Not having commenced manfully to control his thoughts, he is not in a position to control affairs and to adopt serious responsibilities. He is not fit to act independently and stand alone, but he is limited only by the thoughts which he chooses.

There can be no progress, no achievement without sacrifice. A man's worldly success will be in the measure that he sacrifices his confused animal thoughts, and fixes his mind on the development of his plans, and the strengthening of his resolution and self-reliance. And the higher he lifts his thoughts, the more manly, upright, and righteous he becomes, the greater will be his success, the more blessed and enduring will be his achievements.

The universe does not favor the greedy, the dishonest, the vicious, although on the mere surface it may sometimes appear to do so; it helps the honest, the magnanimous, the virtuous. All the great Teachers of the ages have declared this in varying forms, and to prove and know it a man has but to persist in making himself more and more virtuous by lifting up his thoughts.

Intellectual achievements are the result of thought consecrated to the search for knowledge, or for the beautiful and true in life and nature. Such achievements may be sometimes connected with vanity and ambition, but they are not the outcome of those characteristics. They are the natural outgrowth of long and arduous effort, and of pure and unselfish thoughts.

Spiritual achievements are the consummation of holy aspirations. He who lives constantly in the conception of noble and lofty thoughts, who dwells upon all that is pure and unselfish, will, as surely as the sun reaches its zenith and the moon its full, become wise and noble in character, and rise into a position of influence and blessedness.

Achievement, of whatever kind, is the crown of effort, the diadem of thought. By the aid of self-control, resolution, purity, righteousness, and well-directed thought a man ascends. By the aid of animality, indolence, impurity, corruption, and confusion of thought a man descends.

A man may rise to high success in the world, and even to lofty altitudes in the spiritual realm, and again descend into weakness and wretchedness by allowing arrogant, selfish, and corrupt thoughts to take possession of him.

Victories attained by right thought can only be maintained by watchfulness. Many give way when success is assured, and rapidly fall back into failure.

All achievements, whether in the business, intellectual, or spiritual world, are the result of definitely directed thought, are governed by the same law and are of the same method; the only difference lies in *the object of attainment*.

He who would accomplish little must sacrifice little. He who would achieve much must sacrifice much. He who would attain highly must sacrifice greatly.

Visions and Ideals

The dreamers are the saviors of the world. As the visible world is sustained by the invisible, so men, through all their trials and sins and sordid vocations, are nourished by the beautiful visions of their solitary dreamers. Humanity cannot forget its dreamers. It cannot let their ideals fade and die. It lives in them. It knows them as the *realities* which it shall one day see and know.

Composer, sculptor, painter, poet, prophet, sage, these are the makers of the afterworld, the architects of heaven. The world is beautiful because they have lived; without them, laboring humanity would perish.

He who cherishes a beautiful vision, a lofty ideal in his heart, will one day realize it. Columbus cherished a vision of another world, and he discovered it. Copernicus fostered the vision of a multiplicity of worlds and a wider universe, and he revealed it. Buddha beheld the vision of a spiritual world of stainless beauty and perfect peace, and he entered into it.

Cherish your visions. Cherish your ideals. Cherish the music that stirs in your heart, the beauty that forms in your mind, the loveliness that drapes your purest thoughts, for out of them will grow all delightful conditions, all heavenly environment; of these, if you but remain true to them, your world will at last be built.

To desire is to obtain; to aspire is to achieve. Shall man's basest desires receive the fullest measure of gratification, and his purest aspirations starve for lack of sustenance? Such is not the Law. Such a condition of things can never obtain—"Ask and receive."

Dream lofty dreams, and as you dream, so shall you become. Your Vision is the promise of what you shall one day be. Your Ideal is the prophecy of what you shall at last unveil.

The greatest achievement was at first and for a time a dream. The oak sleeps in the acorn; the bird waits in the egg; and in the highest vision of the soul a waking angel stirs. Dreams are the seedlings of realities.

Your circumstances may be uncongenial, but they shall not long remain so if you but perceive an Ideal and strive to reach it. You cannot travel *within* and stand still *without.* Here is a youth hard pressed by poverty and labor; confined long hours in an unhealthy workshop; unschooled, and lacking all the arts of refinement. But he dreams of better things. He thinks of intelligence, of refinement, of grace and beauty. He conceives of, mentally builds up, an ideal condition of life. The vision of a wider liberty and a larger scope takes possession of him; unrest urges him to action, and he utilizes all his spare time and means, small though they are, to the development of his latent powers and resources.

Very soon, so altered has his mind become, that the workshop can no longer hold him. It has become so out of harmony with his mentality that it falls out of his life as a garment is cast aside, and, with the growth of opportunities which fit the scope of his expanding powers, he passes out of it forever.

Years later we see this youth as a full-grown man. We find him a master of certain forces of the mind which he wields with world-wide influence and almost unequaled power. In his hands he holds the cords of gigantic responsibilities. He speaks, and lo! lives are changed. Men and women hang upon his words and remold their characters, and, sunlike, he becomes the fixed and luminous center around which innumerable destinies revolve. He has realized the Vision of his youth. He has become one with his Ideal.

And you, too, youthful reader, will realize the Vision (not the idle wish) of your heart, be it base or beautiful, or a mixture of both, for you will always gravitate toward that which you secretly most love. Into your hands will be placed the exact results of your own thoughts; you will receive that which you earn, no more, no less. Whatever your present environment may be, you will fall, remain, or rise with your thoughts, your Vision, your Ideal. You will become as small as your controlling desire; as great as your dominant aspiration. In the beautiful words of Stanton Kirkham Davis, "You may be keeping accounts, and presently you shall walk out of the door that for so long has seemed to you the barrier of your ideals, and shall find yourself before an audience—the pen still behind your ear, the ink stains on your fingers—and then and there shall pour out the torrent of your inspiration. You may be driving sheep, and you shall wander to the city—bucolic and open mouthed; shall wander under the intrepid guidance of the spirit into the studio of the master, and after a time he shall say, 'I have nothing more to teach you.' And now you have become the master, who did so recently dream of great things while driving sheep. You shall lay down the saw and the plane to take upon yourself the regeneration of the world."

The thoughtless, the ignorant, and the indolent, seeing only the apparent effects of things and not the things themselves, talk of luck, of fortune, and chance. Seeing a man grow rich, they say, "How lucky he is!" Observing another become intellectual, they exclaim, "How highly favored he is!" And noting the saintly character and wide influence of another, they remark, "How chance aids him at every turn!"

They do not see the trials and failures and struggles which these men have voluntarily encountered in order to gain their experience. They have no knowledge of the sacrifices they have made, of the undaunted efforts they have put forth, of the faith they have exercised, that they might overcome the apparently insurmountable, and realize the Vision of their heart. They do not know the darkness and the heartaches; they only see the light and joy, and call it "luck"; do not see the long and arduous journey, but only behold the pleasant goal, and call it "good fortune"; do not understand the process, but only perceive the result, and call it "chance."

In all human affairs there are *efforts,* and there are *results,* and the strength of the effort is the measure of the result. Chance is not. "Gifts," powers, material, intellectual, and spiritual possessions are the fruits of effort. They are thoughts completed, objects accomplished, visions realized.

The Vision that you glorify in your mind, the Ideal that you enthrone in your heart—this you will build your life by, this you will become.

Serenity

Calmness of mind is one of the beautiful jewels of wisdom. It is the result of long and patient effort in self-control. Its presence is an indication of ripened experience, and of a more than ordinary knowledge of the laws and operations of thought.

A man becomes calm in the measure that he understands himself as a thought-evolved being, for such knowledge necessitates the understanding of others as the result of thought. As he develops a right understanding, and sees more and more clearly the internal relations of things by the action of cause and effect, he ceases to fuss and fume and worry and grieve, and remains poised, steadfast, serene.

The calm man, having learned how to govern himself, knows how to adapt himself to others; and they, in turn, reverence his spiritual strength, and feel that they can learn of him and rely upon him. The more tranquil a man becomes, the greater is his success, his influence, his power for good. Even the ordinary trader will find his business prosperity increase as he develops a greater self-control and equanimity, for people will always prefer to deal with a man whose demeanor is strongly equable.

The strong calm man is always loved and revered. He is like a shade-giving tree in a thirsty land, or a sheltering rock in a storm. "Who does not love a tranquil heart, a sweet-tempered, balanced life? It does not matter whether it rains or shines, or what changes come to those possessing these blessings, for they are always sweet, serene, and calm. That exquisite poise of character which we call serenity is the last lesson of culture; it is the flowering of life, the fruitage of the soul. It is precious as wisdom, more to be desired than gold—yea, than even fine gold. How insignificant mere money-seeking looks in comparison with a serene life—a life that dwells in the ocean of Truth, beneath the waves, beyond the reach of tempests, in the Eternal Calm!"

"How many people we know who sour their lives, who ruin all that is sweet and beautiful by explosive tempers, who destroy their poise of character, and make bad blood! It is a question whether the great majority of people do not ruin their lives and mar their happiness by lack of self-control. How few people we meet in life who are well-balanced, who have that exquisite poise which is characteristic of the finished character!"

Yes, humanity surges with uncontrolled passion, is tumultuous with ungoverned grief, is blown about by anxiety and doubt. Only the wise man, only he whose thoughts are controlled and purified, makes the winds and the storms of the soul obey him.

Tempest-tossed souls, wherever ye may be, under whatsoever conditions ye may live, know this—in the ocean of life the isles of Blessedness are smiling, and the sunny shore of your ideal awaits your coming. Keep your hand firmly upon the helm of thought. In the bark of your soul reclines the commanding Master; He does but sleep; wake Him. Self-control is strength; Right Thought is mastery; Calmness is power.

Say unto your heart, "Peace, be still!"

Staying the Course in Right Thinking

by Mel B.

As A Man Thinketh will certainly change the life of any person who develops a new way of thinking. It is exciting to discover that you can change your life in this way, and at first one can almost be carried away by the novelty of this new discovery. But what happens later? Will this early confidence and optimism survive and grow into something even better? How will this changed outlook fare over time and in facing the problems and challenges that come to everybody in some form?

A typical experience is to make progress in occasional spurts accompanied by a few setbacks and disappointments. Our human need in any situation is to outline the results we desire and then to feel hurt and betrayed if those results don't appear as planned. We must also face the unpleasant fact that our human tendency is to want what we want when we want it, without regard for the way our desires may collide with the interests and rights of others or how much time real change actually takes. Allen, in writing *As A Man Thinketh*, was only stating and describing the existence of a Great Law, but he also believed that thought can be destructive if wrongly applied. In viewing the often-tragic course of human affairs, we can see how true this is.

There is now a large body of user-friendly literature to support and reinforce our thought lives as we seek improvement. One of the best and oldest is Ralph Waldo Trine's *In Tune with the Infinite*, which in 1914 reportedly had a major role in giving auto pioneer Henry Ford the confidence to push ahead with his plans for an expanded company. Another great book is Emmet Fox's *Power Through Constructive Thinking*, which was then followed by Norman Vincent Peale's 1952 blockbuster, *The Power of Positive Thinking*. The underlying point in these books, and numerous similar publications, is that we shape our lives by the thoughts we choose, and also that we are children of a Loving God who works along with us. But how do these fit in with continued practice of the AA program?

One important rule is to accept such books as supplements for AA literature, but not as replacements. The best way to safeguard sobriety is to read the conference-approved AA literature, attend meetings regularly, and follow the Twelve Steps in daily living. There is certainly time, however, for additional inspirational literature as one faces new problems in everyday living. If this reading is compatible with what one finds in AA, it can only enhance and explain truth as we continue to discover it.

As a rule, however, most of us cannot find quick fixes for longstanding problems or perform miracles that are usually beyond human capabilities. But many problems will dissolve over time if they are dealt with on a daily basis, using the spiritual tools offered in the program. When this happens, we can look back and see how small amounts of progress eventually brought important breakthroughs in our lives. If we seek truth and growth in a spiritual way, we will find it, and along the way, we will help others find progress in their own lives. As with following the AA program, the person seeking self-improvement should keep three things in mind: (1) Continue, (2) Continue, (3) Continue.

Part Two
Henry Drummond

Drummond's Great Message on Love

by Mel B.

According to AA's authorized biography of co-founder Dr. Bob S., he put a lot of stock in Henry Drummond's *The Greatest Thing in the World*, a talk given in 1887. One early member said that he advised her to get it for a woman who was going into D.T.'s. "He told me to give her the medication, and he said, 'When she comes out of it and she decides she wants to be a different woman, get her [this book]. Tell her to read it through every day for 30 days, and she'll be a different woman.'"

Dr. Bob's confidence in Drummond's classic may be why I found it on an early list of recommended books for AA members. Later on, I found copies on sale at groups in the Detroit area. This may have also reflected Dr. Bob's influence, because Detroit AA founder Archie T., during his early recovery, had spent almost a year with Dr. Bob in Akron. I'm sure the book inspired a number of our pioneer members who went on to do great work in AA at the local level and to maintain sobriety all their lives.

What was its special appeal for AA members? I believe it struck a responsive chord in early AA because it brought Love home to everyday living. Love, instead of being an unattainable something floating up in the sky, is a force that must be expressed in one's daily living if it is to have any real effect. Using St. Paul's great statement on Love from I Corinthians 13, Drummond shows how it has nine key virtues which any person can learn and practice: Patience, Kindness, Generosity, Humility, Courtesy, Unselfishness, Good Temper, Guilelessness, and Sincerity.

It's not difficult to understand why these would be important virtues for alcoholics to consider. In my own life as a compulsive drinker, I was deficient in all of them. It's also likely that some of these great virtues appeared to me as *weaknesses*. There may have been times when I was able to take advantage of people who were unusually patient and kind, and I was completely unacquainted with the importance of such qualities as unselfishness, good temper and guilelessness.

Drummond, in his great talk, analyzed Love, contrasted it with other important things, and then defended it as the one thing really worth having. One important point he made is that Love is the only thing that really lasts; everything else we know today will pass away. He gave the talk at a time when wonderful new inventions and discoveries were coming on stream, but he warned that all of these would be superseded by additional discoveries and changes. We can find proof of this simply by reflecting how greatly things have changed since 1887, and also by realizing that our descendants a century from now will be looking at our present age in much the same way we view the nineteenth century.

In any case, Drummond's list of the nine ingredients are made to order for recovering people. AA co-founder Bill W. repeatedly targeted the mad pursuit of money, power and prestige as among the demons that had almost destroyed him and continued as threats to the individual alcoholic and AA as a society. As he saw it, getting free of alcohol was only the start of one's quest for happiness and real stability. "At the beginning, we sacrificed alcohol," he wrote in 1955. "We had to, or it would have killed us. But we couldn't get rid of alcohol unless we made other sacrifices. Big-shotism and phony thinking had to go. We had to toss self-justification, self-pity, and anger right out the window. We had to quit the crazy contest for personal prestige and big bank balances. We had to take personal responsibility for our sorry state and quit blaming others for it."[2]

It hardly needs stating that anyone caught up in big-shotism and phony thinking would be woefully deficient in most of the nine ingredients of Love cited in Drummond's masterpiece. And while active alcoholism caused most of us to fail in our pursuit of money, power and prestige, the real block to true spiritual growth was that these goals continued to dominate our thinking, even in recovery. In fact, with drunkenness no longer blocking the way, the temptation is strong to seek expression and fulfillment in worldly pursuits.

This is when Drummond's little book can become a virtual lifesaver for the recovering person. All along, the big mistake confronting the world has been making gods of lesser things rather than becoming devoted to God as Love. These lesser things may be suitable for certain purposes, but we have deeper needs that they can never touch. As a crude example, I can cite the thrilling experience of getting a new car after being sober for about a year. This was a giant leap forward for a person who had previously been either destitute or dependent. So for a short time, the car seemed to give me prestige and self-importance, along with some of the big-shotism that can be any alcoholic's downfall. I quickly got over this phase, but I haven't given up owning automobiles as convenient vehicles for personal transportation. Such material possessions can be properly viewed as gifts from God, but they should never replace God or be a substitute for the Grace we really need in our lives.

How do we know when we're finding and expressing *real* Love and not the many counterfeits that seem to be circulating? Using Drummond's talk as a guide, we only have to check ourselves on any of the nine ingredients of Love. We can work to feel and express more patience, more kindness, more unselfishness, and more of all the other things that constitute Love. And as we do so, we are moving closer to God in thought and feeling.

Drummond's talk also contains warnings for persons who feel they are on a true spiritual path. He notes that Christian work gives little protection against unchristian feeling. Translated to the AA situation, we can see that even our good AA work does not protect us from jealousy of other members or undue pride in length of sobriety and other accomplishments. And we have to be very devoted AA members indeed to avoid feeling critical of the person who repeatedly fails to find sobriety in the program. It is all too easy to fall in the trap of self-righteousness and condemnation. But when we do, we lose out in finding the priceless gift of Love that Drummond describes.

While *The Greatest Thing in the World* may sound impractical and idealistic, I have found it highly useful in addressing the everyday problems of life. I once spent an evening with a young salesman who was failing in his work and also in getting along with others in the organization. He was actually suffering from several problems which are bound to be fatal to a sales career. He had great pride in his high intelligence, he was probably suspicious of others and hostile towards competitors, and he was extremely ambitious. These problems were actually expressing as pride, anger and greed, three of the seven deadly sins. By admitting these problems and dealing with them, he actually became a competent, successful salesman and found his true place in business. I was never able to determine if our talk and Drummond's book had been key factors in his changed life, but it certainly helped give him new insights.

I'm sure this is the value that Dr. Bob S. found in Drummond's writing. In his personal story, he conceded that selfishness may have had an important part in bringing on his alcoholism. He also suffered from false pride which he finally had to deal with in accepting the program and making amends to people he had harmed. *The Greatest Thing in the World* is the perfect prescription for people suffering from pride and selfishness—a population that includes a fair number of recovering persons. If we seek first the Supreme Gift of Love, all of the other things we thought we needed may be added to us. And we will move towards freedom from the self-imposed tyranny of worldly pursuits.

Who Was Henry Drummond?

by Mel B.

Famous in his time, Henry Drummond would be completely forgotten today except for *The Greatest Thing in the World*, a talk delivered in 1887 at a religious conference in Northfield, Massachusetts. He was best known in his lifetime for *Natural Law in the Spiritual World,* a brilliant but failed effort to settle the growing conflict between religion and science. His other writings brought him further acclaim, and he was highly regarded as a professor, lecturer, author, scientist and philosopher.

Drummond was born near Stirling, Scotland, on August 17, 1861. He was educated at the Universities of Edinburgh and Tübingen and later became professor of Natural Science at the College of the Free Church of Scotland. He traveled extensively in Australia and the Far East and also made trips to the Rocky Mountains and Central Africa.

Despite his remarkable achievements, Drummond's true devotion was to the spiritual realm, and friends noted his inherent goodness and kind nature. "Drummond was a man 'who lived it,'" a friend said. "His face was an index to his inner life. All the time we were together he was a Christlike man and a rebuke to me."

The great turning point in Drummond's life was in the early 1870s, when he and other young men of his class attended the great revivals held in England and Scotland by evangelist Dwight L. Moody. Moody was a homespun, relatively unlettered preacher who nonetheless had the ability to sway large audiences and bring thousands to a tearful repentance. His basic non-intellectualism should have driven Drummond away. Instead, they became close friends, and Drummond came to Moody's Northfield Conferences in Massachusetts as an invited speaker. Moody, hearing *The Greatest Thing in the World,* recommended it for immediate publication by his brother-in-law, Fleming Revell. It has remained in print ever since, an inspiration to persons of all faiths.

The Greatest Thing in the World

by Henry Drummond

A talk given in 1887

Paul's Great Message: I Corinthians 13

[Henry Drummond began his talk by reading aloud to his audience all of Chapter 13 of the Apostle Paul's First Letter to the Corinthians.]

"Though I speak with the tongues of men and of angels, and have not Love, I am become as sounding brass, or a tinkling cymbal. And though I have the gift of prophecy, and understand all mysteries, and all knowledge; and though I have all Faith, so that I could remove mountains, and have not Love, I am nothing. And though I bestow all my goods to feed the poor, and though I give my body to be burned, and have not Love, it profiteth me nothing.

"Love suffereth long, and is kind;
Love envieth not;
Love vaunteth not itself, is not puffed up,
Doth not behave itself unseemly,
Seeketh not her own,
Is not easily provoked,
Thinketh no evil;
Rejoiceth not in iniquity, but rejoiceth in the truth;
Beareth all things, believeth all things, hopeth all things,
endureth all things.

"Love never faileth: but whether there be prophecies, they shall fail; whether there be tongues, they shall cease; whether there be knowledge, it shall vanish away. For we know in part, and we prophesy in part. But when that which is perfect is come, then that which is in part shall be done away.

"When I was a child, I spake as a child, I understood as a child, I thought as a child: but when I became a man, I put away childish things.

For now we see through a glass, darkly; but then face to face: now I know in part; but then shall I know even as also I am known. And now abideth Faith, Hope, and Love, these three; but the greatest of these is Love."

The Greatest Thing in the World

Every one has asked himself the great question of antiquity as of the modern world: What is the *summum bonum*—the supreme good? You have life before you. Once only you can live it. What is the noblest object of desire, the supreme gift to covet?

We have been accustomed to be told that the greatest thing in the religious world is Faith. That great word has been the key-note for centuries of the popular religion; and we have easily learned to look upon it as the greatest thing in the world. Well, we are wrong. If we have been told that, we may miss the mark. I have taken you, in the chapter which I have just read, to Christianity at its source; and there we have seen, "The greatest of these is Love." It is not an oversight. Paul was speaking of faith just a moment before. He says, "If I have all Faith, so that I can remove mountains, and have not Love: I am nothing." So far from forgetting, he deliberately contrasts them, "Now abideth Faith, Hope, Love," and without a moment's hesitation the decision falls, "The greatest of these is Love."

And it is not prejudice. A man is apt to recommend to others his own strong point.

Love was not Paul's strong point. The observing student can detect a beautiful tenderness growing and ripening all through his character as Paul gets old; but the hand that wrote "The greatest of these is Love," when we meet it first, is stained with blood.

Nor is this letter to the Corinthians peculiar in singling out Love as the *summum bonum*. The masterpieces of Christianity are agreed about it. Peter says, "Above all things have fervent love among yourselves." Above *all things*. And John goes farther, "God is love." And you remember the profound remark which Paul makes elsewhere, "Love is the fulfilling of the law." Did you ever think what he meant by that? In those days men were working their passage to Heaven by keeping the Ten Commandments, and the hundred and ten other commandments which they had manufactured out of them. Christ said, I will show you a more simple way. If you do one thing, you will do these hundred and ten things, without ever thinking about them. If you love, you will unconsciously fulfill the whole law. And you can readily see for yourselves how that must be so. Take any of the commandments. "Thou shalt have no other gods before Me." If a man love God, you will not require to tell him that. Love is the fulfilling of that law. "Take not His name in vain." Would he ever dream of taking His name in vain if he loved Him? "Remember the Sabbath day to keep it holy." Would he not be too glad to have one day in seven to dedicate more exclusively to the object of his affection? Love would fulfill all these laws regarding God. And so, if he loved Man you would never think of telling him to honor his father and mother. He could not do anything else. It would be preposterous to tell him not to kill. You could only insult him if you suggested that he should not steal—how could he steal from those he loved? It would be superfluous to beg him not to bear false witness against his neighbor. If he loved him it would be the last thing he would do.

And you would never dream of urging him not to covet what his neighbors had. He would rather they possessed it than himself. In this way, "Love is the fulfilling of the law." It is the rule for fulfilling all rules, the new commandment for keeping all the old commandments, Christ's one secret of the Christian life.

Now Paul had learned that; and in this noble eulogy he has given us the most wonderful and original account extant of the *summum bonum*. We may divide it into three parts. In the beginning of the short chapter, we have Love *contrasted*; in the heart of it, we have Love *analyzed*; towards the end we have Love *defended* as the supreme gift.

The Contrast

Paul begins by contrasting Love with other things that men in those days thought much of. I shall not attempt to go over those things in detail. Their inferiority is already obvious.

He contrasts it with eloquence. And what a noble gift it is, the power of playing upon the souls and wills of men, and rousing them to lofty purposes and holy deeds. Paul says, "If I speak with the tongues of men and of angels, and have not love, I am become as sounding brass, or a tinkling cymbal." And we all know why. We have all felt the brazenness of words without emotion, the hollowness, the unaccountable unpersuasiveness, of eloquence behind which lies no Love.

He contrasts it with property. He contrasts it with mysteries. He contrasts it with faith. He contrasts it with charity. Why is Love greater than faith? Because the end is greater than the means. And why is it greater than charity? Because the whole is greater than the part. Love is greater than faith, because the end is greater than the means. What is the use of having faith? It is to connect the soul with God. And what is the object of connecting man with God? That he may become like God. But God is Love. Hence Faith, the means, is in order to Love, the end. Love, therefore, obviously is greater than faith.

It is greater than charity, again, because the whole is greater than a part. Charity is only a little bit of Love, one of the innumerable avenues of Love, and there may even be, and there is a great deal of charity without Love. It is a very easy thing to toss a copper to a beggar on the street; it is generally an easier thing than not to do it. Yet Love is just as often in the withholding. We purchase relief from the sympathetic feelings roused by the spectacle of misery, at the copper's cost. It is too cheap—too cheap for us, and often too dear for the beggar. If we really loved him we would either do more for him, or less.

Then Paul contrasts it with sacrifice and martyrdom. And I beg the little band of would-be missionaries—and I have the honor to call some of you by this name for the first time—to remember that though you give your bodies to be burned, and have not Love, it profits nothing—nothing! You can take nothing greater to the heathen world than the impress and reflection of the Love of God upon your own character. That is the universal language. It will take you years to speak in Chinese, or in the dialects of India. From the day you land, that language of Love, understood by all, will be pouring forth its unconscious eloquence. It is the man who is the missionary, it is not his words. His character is his message.

In the heart of Africa, among the great Lakes, I have come across black men and women who remembered the only white man they ever saw before—David Livingstone; and as you cross his footsteps in that dark continent, men's faces light up as they speak of the kind Doctor who passed there years ago. They could not understand him; but they felt the Love that beat in his heart. Take into your new sphere of labor, where you also mean to lay down your life, that simple charm, and your lifework must succeed. You can take nothing greater, you need take nothing less. It is not worth while going if you take anything less. You may take every accomplishment; you may be braced for every sacrifice; but if you give your body to be burned, and have not Love, it will profit you and the cause of Christ nothing.

The Analysis

After contrasting Love with these things, Paul, in three verses, very short, gives us an amazing analysis of what this supreme thing is. I ask you to look at it. It is a compound thing, he tells us. It is like light. As you have seen a man of science take a beam of light and pass it through a crystal prism, as you have seen it come out on the other side of the prism broken up into its component colors—red, and blue, and yellow, and violet, and orange, and all the colors of the rainbow—so Paul passes this thing, Love, through the magnificent prism of his inspired intellect, and it comes out on the other side broken up into its elements.

And in these few words we have what one might call the Spectrum of Love, the analysis of Love. Will you observe what its elements are? Will you notice that they have common names; that they are virtues which we hear about every day; that they are things which can be practiced by every man in every place in life; and how, by a multitude of small things and ordinary virtues, the supreme thing, the *summum bonum*, is made up?

The spectrum of Love has nine ingredients:

Patience—"Love suffereth long."
Kindness—"And is kind."
Generosity—"Love envieth not."
Humility—"Love vaunteth not itself, is not puffed up."
Courtesy—"Doth not behave itself unseemly."
Unselfishness—"Seeketh not her own."
Good Temper—"Is not easily provoked."
Guilelessness—"Thinketh no evil."
Sincerity—"Rejoiceth not in iniquity, but rejoiceth in the truth."

Patience; kindness; generosity; humility; courtesy; unselfishness; good temper; guilelessness; sincerity—these make up the supreme gift, the stature of the perfect man. You will observe that all are in relation to men, in relation to life, in relation to the known today and the near tomorrow, and not to the unknown eternity. We hear much of Love to God; Christ spoke much of love to man. We make a great deal of peace with heaven; Christ made much of peace on earth. Religion is not a strange or added thing, but the inspiration of the secular life, the breathing of an eternal spirit through this temporal world. The supreme thing, in short, is not a thing at all, but the giving of a further finish to the multitudinous words and acts which make up the sum of every common day.

There is no time to do more than make a passing note upon each of these ingredients.

Patience

Love is *Patience*. This is the normal attitude of Love; Love passive, Love waiting to begin; not in a hurry; calm; ready to do its work when the summons comes, but meantime wearing the ornament of a meek and quiet spirit. Love suffers long; beareth all things; believeth all things; hopeth all things. For Love understands, and therefore waits.

Kindness

Love active. Have you ever noticed how much of Christ's life was spent in doing kind things—in *merely* doing kind things? Run over it with that in view, and you will find that He spent a great proportion of His time simply in making people happy, in doing good turns to people.

There is only one thing greater than happiness in the world, and that is holiness; and it is not in our keeping; but what God *has* put in our power is the happiness of those about us, and that is largely to be secured by our being kind to them.

"The greatest thing," says someone,"a man can do for his Heavenly Father is to be kind to some of His other children." I wonder why it is that we are not all kinder than we are? How much the world needs it. How easily it is done. How instantaneously it acts. How infallibly it is remembered. How super abundantly it pays itself back—for there is no debtor in the world so honorable, so superbly honorable, as Love. "Love never faileth." Love is success, Love is happiness, Love is life. "Love," I say, with Browning, "is energy of Life."

> For life, with all it yields of joy or woe
> And hope and fear,
> Is just our chance o' the prize of learning love—
> How love might be, hath been indeed, and is.

Where Love is, God is. He that dwelleth in Love dwelleth in God. God is Love. Therefore *love*. Without distinction, without calculation, without procrastination, love. Lavish it upon the poor, where it is very easy; especially upon the rich, who often need it most; most of all upon our equals, where it is very difficult, and for whom perhaps we each do least of all.

There is a difference between *trying to please* and *giving pleasure*. Give pleasure. Lose no chance of giving pleasure. For that is the ceaseless and anonymous triumph of a truly loving spirit. "I shall pass through this world but once. Any good thing therefore that I can do, or any kindness that I can show to any human being, let me do it now. Let me not defer or neglect it, for I shall not pass this way again."

Generosity

"Love envieth not." This is Love in competition with others. Whenever you attempt a good work you will find other men doing the same kind of work, and probably doing it better. Envy them not. Envy is a feeling of ill-will to those who are in the same line as ourselves, a spirit of covetousness and detraction. How little Christian work even is a protection against un-Christian feeling. That most despicable of all the unworthy moods which cloud a Christian's soul assuredly waits for us on the threshold of every work, unless we are fortified with this grace of magnanimity. Only one thing truly need the Christian envy, the large, rich, generous soul which "envieth not."

And then, after having learned all that, you have to learn this further thing.

Humility

Humility—to put a seal upon your lips and forget what you have done. After you have been kind, after Love has stolen forth into the world and done its beautiful work, go back into the shade again and say nothing about it. Love hides even from itself. Love waives even self-satisfaction. "Love vaunteth not itself, is not puffed up."

Courtesy

The fifth ingredient is a somewhat strange one to find in this *summum bonum:* Courtesy. This is Love in society, Love in relation to etiquette. "Love doth not behave itself unseemly." Politeness has been defined as love in trifles. Courtesy is said to be love in little things. And the one secret of politeness is to love. Love *cannot* behave itself unseemly. You can put the most untutored person into the highest society, and if they have a reservoir of Love in their heart, they will not behave themselves unseemly. They simply cannot do it.

Carlyle said of Robert Burns that there was no truer gentleman in Europe than the ploughman-poet. It was because he loved everything—the mouse, and the daisy, and all the things, great and small, that God had made. So with this simple passport he could mingle with any society, and enter courts and palaces from his little cottage on the banks of the Ayr. You know the meaning of the word "gentleman." It means a gentle man—a man who does things gently, with love. And that is the whole art and mystery of it. The gentle man cannot in the nature of things do an ungentle, an ungentlemanly thing. The ungentle soul, the inconsiderate, unsympathetic nature cannot do anything else. "Love doth not behave itself unseemly."

Unselfishness

"Love seeketh not her own." Observe: Seeketh not even that which is her own. In Britain the Englishman is devoted, and rightly, to his rights. But there come times when a man may exercise even the higher right of giving up his rights. Yet Paul does not summon us to give up our rights. Love strikes much deeper. It would have us not seek them at all, ignore them, eliminate the personal element altogether from our calculations.

It is not hard to give up our rights. They are often external. The difficult thing is to give up ourselves. The more difficult thing still is not to seek things for ourselves at all. After we have sought them, bought them, won them, deserved them, we have taken the cream off them for ourselves already. Little cross then to give them up. But not to seek them, to look, every man, not on his own things, but on the things of others—*id opus est*.

"Seekest thou great things for thyself?" said the prophet; *"seek them not."* Why? Because there is no greatness in *things*. Things cannot be great. The only greatness is unselfish love. Even self-denial in itself is nothing, is almost a mistake. Only a great purpose or a mightier love can justify the waste. It is more difficult, I have said, not to seek our own at all, than, having sought it, to give it up. I must take that back. It is only true of a partly selfish heart. Nothing is a hardship to Love, and nothing is hard. I believe that Christ's "yoke" is easy, Christ's "yoke" is just His way of taking life. And I believe it is an easier way than any other. I believe it is a happier way than any other.

The most obvious lesson in Christ's teaching is that there is no happiness in having and getting anything, but only in giving. I repeat, *there is no happiness in having or getting, but only in giving*. And half the world is on the wrong scent in the pursuit of happiness. They think it consists in having and getting, and in being served by others. It consists in giving, and in serving others. He that would be great among you, said Christ, let him serve. He that would be happy, let him remember that there is but one way—it is more blessed, it is more happy, to give than to receive.

The next ingredient is a very remarkable one:

Good Temper

"Love is not easily provoked." Nothing could be more striking than to find this here. We are inclined to look upon bad temper as a very harmless weakness. We speak of it as a mere infirmity of nature, a family failing, a matter of temperament, not a thing to take into very serious account in estimating a man's character. And yet here, right in the heart of this analysis of Love, it finds a place; and the Bible again and again returns to condemn it as one of the most destructive elements in human nature.

The peculiarity of ill temper is that it is the vice of the virtuous. It is often the one blot on an otherwise noble character. You know men who are all but perfect, and women who would be entirely perfect, but for an easily ruffled, quick-tempered, or "touchy" disposition. This compatibility of ill temper with high moral character is one of the strangest and saddest problems of ethics. The truth is there are two great classes of sins—sins of the *Body,* and sins of the Disposition. The Prodigal Son may be taken as a type of the first, the Elder Brother of the second [Luke 15:11-32]. Now, society has no doubt whatever as to which of these is the worse. Its brand falls, without a challenge, upon the Prodigal.

But are we right? We have no balance to weigh one another's sins, and coarser and finer are but human words; but faults in the higher nature may be less venial than those in the lower, and to the eye of Him who is Love, a sin against Love may seem a hundred times more base. No form of vice, not worldliness, not greed of gold, not drunkenness itself, does more to un-Christianize society than evil temper. For embittering life, for breaking up communities, for destroying the most sacred relationships, for devastating homes, for withering up men and women, for taking the bloom off childhood; in short, for sheer gratuitous misery-producing power, this influence stands alone.

Look at the Elder Brother, moral, hard-working, patient, dutiful—let him get all credit for his virtues—look at this man, this baby, sulking outside his own father's door. "He was angry," we read, "and would not go in."

Look at the effect upon the father, upon the servants, upon the happiness of the guests. Judge of the effect upon the Prodigal—and how many prodigals are kept out of the Kingdom of God by the unlovely characters of those who profess to be inside?

Analyze, as a study in temper, the thunder-cloud itself as it gathers upon the Elder Brother's brow. What is it made of? Jealousy, anger, pride, uncharity, cruelty, self-righteousness, touchiness, doggedness, sullenness—these are the ingredients of this dark and loveless soul. In varying proportions, also, these are the ingredients of all ill temper. Judge if such sins of the disposition are not worse to live in, and for others to live with, than sins of the body.

Did Christ indeed not answer the question Himself when He said, "I say unto you, that the publicans and the harlots go into the Kingdom of Heaven before you." There is really no place in Heaven for a disposition like this. A man with such a mood could only make Heaven miserable for all the people in it. Except, therefore, such a man be born again, he cannot, he simply *cannot* enter the Kingdom of Heaven. For it is perfectly certain—and you will not misunderstand me—that to enter Heaven a man must take it with him.

You will see then why Temper is significant. It is not in what it is alone, but in what it reveals. This is why I take the liberty now of speaking of it with such unusual plainness. It is a test for love, a symptom, a revelation of an unloving nature at bottom. It is the intermittent fever which bespeaks unintermittent disease within; the occasional bubble escaping to the surface which betrays some rottenness underneath; a sample of the most hidden products of the soul dropped involuntarily when off one's guard; in a word, the lightning form of a hundred hideous and un-Christian sins. For a want of patience, a want of kindness, a want of generosity, a want of courtesy, a want of unselfishness, are all instantaneously symbolized in one flash of Temper.

Hence it is not enough to deal with the Temper. We must go to the source, and change the inmost nature, and the angry humors will die away of themselves. Souls are made sweet not by taking the acid fluids out, but by putting something in—a great Love, a new Spirit, the Spirit of Christ. Christ, the Spirit of Christ, interpenetrating ours, sweetens, purifies, transforms all. This only can eradicate what is wrong, work a chemical change, renovate and regenerate, and rehabilitate the inner man. Willpower does

Guilelessness and Sincerity

Guilelessness and Sincerity may be dismissed almost with a word. Guilelessness is the grace for suspicious people. And the possession of it is the great secret of personal influence. You will find, if you think for a moment, that the people who influence you are people who believe in you. In an atmosphere of suspicion men shrivel up; but in that atmosphere they expand and find encouragement and educative fellowship.

It is a wonderful thing that here and there in this hard, uncharitable world there should still be left a few rare souls who think no evil. This is the great unworldliness. Love "thinketh no evil," imputes no motive, sees the bright side, puts the best construction on every action. What a delightful state of mind to live in! What a stimulus and benediction even to meet with it for a day! To be trusted is to be saved. And if we try to influence or elevate others, we shall soon see that success is in proportion to their belief of our belief in them. For the respect of another is the first restoration of the self-respect a man has lost; our ideal of what he is becomes to him the hope and pattern of what he may become.

"Love rejoiceth not in iniquity, but rejoiceth in the truth." I have called this *Sincerity* from the words rendered in the Authorized Version by "rejoiceth in the truth." And, certainly, were this the real translation, nothing could be more just. For he who loves will love Truth not less than men. He will rejoice in the Truth—rejoice not in what he has been taught to believe; not in this Church's doctrine or in that; not in this ism or in that ism; but "in *the Truth*." He will accept only what is real; he will strive to get at facts; he will search for *Truth* with a humble and unbiased mind, and cherish whatever he finds at any sacrifice.

But the more literal translation of the Revised Version calls for just such a sacrifice for truth's sake here. For what Paul really meant is, as we there read, "Rejoiceth not in unrighteousness, but rejoiceth with the truth," a quality which probably no one English word—and certainly not *Sincerity*—adequately defines. It includes, perhaps more strictly, the self-restraint which not change men. Time does not change men. Christ does. Therefore "Let that mind be in you which was also in Christ Jesus."

Some of us have not much time to lose. Remember, once more that this is a matter of life or death. I cannot help speaking urgently, for myself, for yourselves. "Whoso shall offend one of these little ones, which believe in me, it were better for him that a millstone were hanged about his neck, and that he were drowned in the depth of the sea." That is to say, it is the deliberate verdict of the Lord Jesus that it is better not to live than not to love. *It is better not to live than not to love.*

refuses to make capital out of others' faults: the charity which delights not in exposing the weakness of others, but "covereth all things"; the sincerity of purpose which endeavors to see things as they are, and rejoices to find them better than suspicion feared or calumny denounced.

Learning and Practicing Love

So much for the analysis of Love. Now the business of our lives is to have these things fitted into our characters. That is the supreme work to which we need to address ourselves in this world, to learn Love. Is life not full of opportunities for learning Love? Every man and woman every day has a thousand of them. The world is not a playground; it is a schoolroom. Life is not a holiday, but an education. And the one eternal lesson for us all is *how better we can love*.

What makes a man a good cricketer? Practice. What makes a man a good artist, a good sculptor, a good musician? Practice. What makes a man a good linguist, a good stenographer? Practice. What makes a man a good man? Practice. Nothing else. There is nothing capricious about religion. We do not get the soul in different ways, under different laws, from those in which we get the body and the mind. If a man does not exercise his arm he develops no biceps muscle; and if a man does not exercise his soul, he acquires no muscle in his soul, no strength of character, no vigor of moral fiber, nor beauty of spiritual growth. Love is not a thing of enthusiastic emotion. It is a rich, strong, manly, vigorous expression of the whole round Christian character—the Christ-like nature in its fullest development. And the constituents of this great character are only to be built up by ceaseless practice.

What was Christ doing in the carpenter's shop? Practicing. Though perfect, we read that He *learned* obedience and grew in wisdom and in favor with God. Do not quarrel therefore with your lot in life. Do not complain of its never-ceasing cares, its petty environment, the vexations you have to stand, the small and sordid souls you have to live and work with. Above all, do not resent temptation, do not be perplexed because it seems to thicken round you more and more, and ceases neither for effort nor for agony nor prayer. That is your practice. That is the practice which God appoints you; and it is having its work in making you patient, and humble, and generous, and unselfish, and kind, and courteous.

Do not grudge the hand that is moulding the still too shapeless image within you. It is growing more beautiful though you see it not, and every touch of temptation may add to its perfection. Therefore keep in the midst of life. Do not isolate yourself. Be among men, and among things, and among troubles, and difficulties, and obstacles. You remember Goethe's words: *Es bildet ein Talent sich in der Stille, doch ein Charakter in dem Strom der Welt.* "Talent develops itself in solitude; character in the stream of life." Talent develops itself in solitude—the talent of prayer, of faith, of meditation, of seeing the unseen; Character grows in the stream of the world's life. That chiefly is where men are to learn love.

How? Now, how? To make it easier, I have named a few of the elements of love. But these are only elements. Love itself can never be defined. Light is something more than the sum of its ingredients—a glowing, dazzling, tremulous ether. And love is something more than all its elements—a palpitating, quivering, sensitive, living thing. By synthesis of all the colors, men can make whiteness, they cannot make light. By synthesis of all the virtues, men can make virtue, they cannot make love.

How then are we to have this transcendent living whole conveyed into our souls? We brace our wills to secure it. We try to copy those who have it. We lay down rules about it. We watch. We pray. But these things alone will not bring Love into our nature. Love is an *effect*. And only as we fulfill the right condition can we have the effect produced. Shall I tell you what the *cause* is?

If you turn to the Revised Version of the First Epistle of John you will find these words: "We love because He first loved us." "We love," not "We love Him." That is the way the old Version has it, and it is quite wrong. *"We love—* because He first loved us." Look at that word "because." It is the cause of which I have spoken. *"Because* He first loved us," the effect follows that we love, we love Him, we love all men. We cannot help it. Because He loved us, we love, we love everybody. Our heart is slowly changed.

Contemplate the love of Christ, and you will love. Stand before that mirror, reflect Christ's character, and you will be changed into the same image from tenderness to tenderness. There is no other way. You cannot love to order. You can only look at the lovely object, and fall in love with it, and grow into likeness to it. And so look at this Perfect Character, this

Perfect Life. Look at the great Sacrifice as He laid down Himself, all through life, and upon the Cross of Calvary, and you must love Him. And loving Him, you must become like Him. Love begets love. It is a process of induction. Put a piece of iron in the presence of an electrified body, and that piece of iron for a time becomes electrified. It is changed into a temporary magnet in the mere presence of a permanent magnet, and as long as you leave the two side by side, they are both magnets alike. Remain side by side with Him who loved us, and gave Himself for us, and you too will become a permanent magnet, a permanently attractive force; and like Him you will draw all men unto you, like Him you will be drawn unto all men. That is the inevitable effect of Love. Any man who fulfills that cause must have that effect produced in him. Try to give up the idea that religion comes to us by chance, or by mystery, or by caprice. It comes to us by natural law, or by supernatural law, for all law is Divine.

Edward Irving went to see a dying boy once, and when he entered the room he just put his hand on the sufferer's head, and said, "My boy, God loves you," and went away. And the boy started from his bed, and called out to the people in the house, "God loves me! God loves me!" It changed that boy. The sense that God loved him overpowered him, melted him down, and began the creating of a new heart in him. And that is how the love of God melts down the unlovely heart in man, and begets in him the new creature, who is patient and humble and gentle and unselfish. And there is no other way to get it. There is no mystery about it. We love others, we love everybody, we love our enemies, because He first loved us.

The Defense

Now I have a closing sentence or two to add about Paul's reason for singling out love as the supreme possession. It is a very remarkable reason. In a single word it is this: *it lasts.* "Love," urges Paul, "never faileth." Then he begins again one of his marvelous lists of the great things of the day, and exposes them one by one. He runs over the things that men thought were going to last, and shows that they were all fleeting, temporary, passing away.

"Whether there be prophecies, they shall fail." It was the mother's ambition for her boy in those days that he should become a prophet. For hundreds of years God had never spoken by means of any prophet, and at that time the prophet was greater than the King. Men waited wistfully for another messenger to come, and hung upon his lips when he appeared as upon the very voice of God. Paul says, "Whether there be prophecies, they shall fail." This book is full of prophecies. One by one they have "failed"; that is, having been fulfilled their work is finished; they have nothing more to do now in the world except to feed a devout man's faith.

Then Paul talks about tongues. That was another thing that was greatly coveted. "Whether there be tongues, they shall cease." As we all know, many, many centuries have passed since tongues have been known in this world. They have ceased. Take it in any sense you like. Take it, for illustration merely, as languages in general—a sense which was not in Paul's mind at all, and which, though it cannot give us the specific lesson, will point the general truth.

Consider the words in which these chapters were written—Greek. It has gone. Take the Latin—the other great tongue of those days. It ceased long ago. Look at the Indian language. It is ceasing. The language of Wales, of Ireland, of the Scottish Highlands is dying before our eyes. The most popular book in the English tongue at the present time, except the Bible, is one of Dickens' works, his *Pickwick Papers*. It is largely written in the language of London street-life; and experts assure us that in fifty years it will be unintelligible to the average English reader.

Knowledge Vanishes Away

Then Paul goes farther, and with even greater boldness adds, "Whether there be knowledge, it shall vanish away." The wisdom of the ancients, where is it? It is wholly gone. A schoolboy today knows more than Sir Isaac Newton knew. His knowledge has vanished away. You put yesterday's newspaper in the fire. Its knowledge has vanished away. You buy the old editions of the great encyclopaedias for a few pence. Their knowledge has vanished away. Look how the coach has been superseded by the use of steam. Look how electricity has superseded that, and swept a hundred almost new inventions into oblivion.

One of the greatest living authorities, Sir William Thomson, said the other day, "The steam-engine is passing away." "Whether there be knowledge, it shall vanish away." At every workshop you will see, in the back yard, a heap of old iron, a few wheels, a few levers, a few cranks, broken and eaten with rust. Twenty years ago that was the pride of the city. Men flocked in from the country to see the great invention; now it is superseded, its day is done. And all the boasted science and philosophy of this day will soon be old.

But yesterday, in the University of Edinburgh, the greatest figure in the faculty was Sir James Simpson, the discoverer of chloroform. The other day his successor and nephew, Professor Simpson, was asked by the librarian of the University to go to the library and pick out the books on his subject that were no longer needed. And his reply to the librarian was this: "Take every textbook that is more than ten years old, and put it down in the cellar." Sir James Simpson was a great authority only a few years ago: men came from all parts of the earth to consult him; and almost the whole teaching of that time is consigned by the science of today to oblivion. And in every branch of science it is the same. "Now we know in part. We see through a glass darkly."

Everlasting Life

Can you tell me anything that is going to last? Many things Paul did not condescend to name. He did not mention money, fortune, fame; but he picked out the great things of his time, the things the best men thought had something in them, and brushed them peremptorily aside. Paul had no charge against these things in themselves. All he said about them was that they would not last. They were great things, but not supreme things. There were things beyond them. What we are stretches past what we do, beyond what we possess.

Many things that men denounce as sins are not sins; but they are temporary. And that is a favorite argument of the New Testament. John says of the world, not that it is wrong, but simply that it "passeth away." There is a great deal in the world that is delightful and beautiful; there is a great deal in it that is great and engrossing; but it will not last. All that is in the world, the lust of the eye, the lust of the flesh, and the pride of life, are but for a little while. Love not the world therefore. Nothing that it contains is worth the life and consecration of an immortal soul. The immortal soul must give itself to something that is immortal. And the only immortal things are these: "Now abideth faith, hope, love, but the greatest of these is love."

Some think the time may come when two of these three things will also pass away—faith into sight, hope into fruition. Paul does not say so. We know but little now about the conditions of the life that is to come. But what is certain is that Love must last. God, the Eternal God, is Love. Covet therefore that everlasting gift, that one thing which it is certain is going to stand, that one coinage which will be current in the Universe when all the other coinages of all the nations of the world shall be useless and unhonored. You will give yourselves to many things; give yourself first to Love. *Hold things in their proportion. Hold things in their proportion.* Let at least the first great object of our lives be to achieve the character defended in these words, the character—and it is the character of Christ—which is built round Love.

I have said this thing is eternal. Did you ever notice how continually John associates love and faith with eternal life? I was not told when I was a boy that "God so loved the world that He gave His only begotten Son, that whosoever believeth in Him should have everlasting life." What I was told, I remember, was, that God so loved the world that, if I trusted in Him, I was to have a thing called peace, or I was to have rest, or I was to have joy, or I was to have safety. But I had to find out for myself that whosoever trusteth in Him—that is, whosoever loveth Him, for trust is only the avenue to Love—hath everlasting *life*.

The Gospel

The Gospel offers a man life. Never offer men a thimbleful of Gospel. Do not offer them merely joy, or merely peace, or merely rest, or merely safety; tell them how Christ came to give men a more abundant life than they have, a life abundant in love and therefore abundant in salvation for themselves, and large in enterprise for the alleviation and redemption of the world. Then only can the Gospel take hold of the whole of a man, body, soul, and spirit, and give to each part of his nature its exercise and reward.

Many of the current Gospels are addressed only to a part of man's nature. They offer peace, not life; faith, not Love; justification, not regeneration. And men slip back again from such religion because it has never really held them. Their nature was not all in it. It offered no deeper and gladder life-current than the life that was lived before. Surely it stands to reason that only a fuller Love can compete with the love of the world.

To love abundantly is to live abundantly, and to love forever is to live forever. Hence, eternal life is inextricably bound up with love. We want to live for ever for the same reason that we want to live tomorrow. Why do you want to live tomorrow? It is because there is some one who loves you, and whom you want to see tomorrow, and be with, and love back. There is no other reason why we should live on than that we love and are beloved. It is when a man has no one to love him that he commits suicide. So long as he has friends, those who love him and whom he loves, he will live; because to live is to love. Be it but the love of a dog, it will keep him in life; but let that go and he has no contact with life, no reason to live. He dies by his own hand.

Knowing God

Eternal life also is to know God, and God is love. This is Christ's own definition. Ponder it. "This is life eternal, that they might know Thee the only true God, and Jesus Christ whom Thou hast sent." Love must be eternal. It is what God is. On the last analysis, then, love is life. Love never faileth, and life never faileth, so long as there is love. That is the philosophy of what Paul is showing us; the reason why in the nature of things Love should be the supreme thing—because it is going to last; because in the nature of things it is an Eternal Life.

It is a thing that we are living now, not that we get when we die; that we shall have a poor chance of getting when we die unless we are living now. No worse fate can befall a man in this world than to live and grow old alone, unloving, and unloved. To be lost is to live in an unregenerate condition, loveless and unloved; and to be saved is to love; and he that dwelleth in love dwelleth already in God. For God is Love.

Read it Ninety Times in Ninety Days

Now I have all but finished. How many of you will join me in reading this chapter once a week for the next three months? A man did that once and it changed his whole life. Will you do it? It is for the greatest thing in the world. You might begin by reading it every day, especially the verses which describe the perfect character. "Love suffereth long, and is kind; love envieth not; love vaunteth not itself." Get these ingredients into your life. Then everything that you do is eternal. It is worth doing. It is worth giving time to. No man can become a saint in his sleep; and to fulfill the condition required demands a certain amount of prayer and meditation and time, just as improvement in any direction, bodily or mental, requires preparation and care.

Address yourselves to that one thing; at any cost have this transcendent character exchanged for yours. You will find as you look back upon your life that the moments that stand out, the moments when you have really lived, are the moments when you have done things in a spirit of Love. As memory scans the past, above and beyond all the transitory pleasures of life, there leap forward those supreme hours when you have been enabled to do unnoticed kindnesses to those round about you, things too trifling to speak about, but which you feel have entered into your eternal life.

I have seen almost all the beautiful things God has made. I have enjoyed almost every pleasure that He has planned for man; and yet as I look back I see standing out above all the life that has gone four or five short experiences when the love of God reflected itself in some poor imitation, some small act of love of mine, and these seem to be the things which alone of all one's life abide. Everything else in all our lives is transitory. Every other good is visionary. But the acts of Love which no man knows about, or can ever know about—they never fail.

Be Not Deceived

In the Book of Matthew [25:31-46], where the Judgement Day is depicted for us in the imagery of One seated upon a throne and dividing the sheep from the goats, the test of a man then is not, "How have I believed?" but "How have I loved?" The test of religion, the final test of religion, is not religiousness, but Love. I say the final test of religion at that great Day is not religiousness, but Love; not what I have done, not what I have believed, not what I have achieved, but how I have discharged the common charities of life.

Sins of commission in that awful indictment are not even referred to. By what we have not done, *by sins of omission,* we are judged. It could not be otherwise. For the withholding of love is the negation of the spirit of Christ, the proof that we never knew Him, that for us He lived in vain. It means that He suggested nothing in all our thoughts, that He inspired nothing in all our lives, that we were not once near enough to Him to be seized with the spell of His compassion for the world. It means that—

> I lived for myself, I thought for myself,
> For myself, and none beside—
> Just as if Jesus had never lived,
> As if He had never died.

It is the Son of *Man* before whom the nations of the world shall be gathered. It is in the presence of *Humanity* that we shall be charged. And the spectacle itself, the mere sight of it, will silently judge each one. Those will be there whom we have met and helped; or there, the unpitied multitude whom we neglected or despised. No other Witness need be summoned. No other charge than lovelessness shall be preferred.

Be not deceived. The words which all of us shall one Day hear, sound not of theology but of life, not of churches and saints but of the hungry and the poor, not of creeds and doctrines but of shelter and clothing, not of Bibles and prayer-books but of cups of cold water in the name of Christ. Thank God the Christianity of today is coming nearer the world's need. Live to help that on. Thank God men know better, by a hairsbreadth, what religion is, what God is, who Christ is, where Christ is. Who is Christ? He who fed the hungry, clothed the naked, visited the sick. And where is Christ? Where?—whoso shall receive a little child in My name receiveth Me. And who are Christ's? Every one that loveth is born of God.

A Final Comment: Timeless Truth about Law and Love

by Mel B.

In these prideful times, it's easily assumed that writings can go into obsolescence along with appliances and fashions. So how can James Allen's brief book from 1908 or Henry Drummond's short talk from 1887 have much relevance in our lives today?

Certain writings from the past will never become outdated because they convey universal truths. Aesop's Fables, for example, speak to every age. It is amazing how many examples from these simple tales are still expressed in our daily language. The same is true of Proverbs and Psalms, the Sermon on the Mount, the Prayer of St. Francis, the aphorisms of Shakespeare—to mention only a few outstanding examples. Even in the space age, we can always benefit from principles that were learned and expressed long ago. This is the Wisdom of the Ages.

Recovering alcoholics in the AA fellowship should understand this because we are the firstborn of what is now called the Twelve Step Movement. The message of the Twelve Steps is that humankind is powerless in the face of certain evils but can find hope and redemption in a spiritual way of life. It matters not what has defeated you; there are times and conditions that are beyond the reach of one's own powers. As the AA Big Book warns, "The alcoholic at certain times has no effective mental defense against the first drink. Except in a few rare cases, neither he nor any other human being can provide such a defense. His defense must come from a Higher Power."[3]

AA, beginning in 1935, became the great instrument for channeling such Higher Power to the suffering alcoholic. Though AA seemed new, the principles it embraced are very old. AA co-founder Bill W. referred to them as "ancient and universal, the common property of mankind."[4] He was saying, of course, that AA and the subsequent Twelve Step program were a new arrangement of principles that had been around for a long time. These principles grow out of two major concepts of God—that God is Law and God is also Love. And the closer we can come to understanding and accepting these spiritual concepts of Law and Love, the closer we'll come to finding the truly abundant Life.

How does God work in our lives as Law? James Allen understood this in a way that should be relevant for any suffering person. The Great Law is that we become what we think, feel and do—this is part of our Free Will. There are no waivers for anybody under this Great Law; it is absolutely no respecter of persons. We can be destroyed by our wrong thoughts and actions, but in the same way we can find hope and recovery; the choice is ours. We would love to find loopholes and escape clauses in the Great Law. Such loopholes and escape clauses can always be discovered in manmade laws, but they are not to be found in the spiritual world. The Great Law is Omnipresent and undeviating, and it never sleeps or can be caught off guard. We have already learned from the natural sciences that the Universe is guided by unbreakable laws, but in the messy and less precise social sciences there has always been the hope that we can construct laws to fit our own whims and delights. So we continue to suffer and fail until the lesson is learned.

But God is also Absolute Love, and we can find this expressed in Drummond's great work based on I Corinthians 13. God's love, as revealed in the life of Jesus, was the blazing passion that burned in Dwight L. Moody and made his revivals world-changing events in the nineteenth century. Drummond, swept up in this outpouring of Grace, became Moody's devoted ally and sought to make peace between science and religion. This failed, partly because the scientific method did not lend itself to the discovery of Universal Love. The twentieth century would bring learned men who would either declare God on life support or pronounce Him dead.

They would have been slower to write the Almighty's obituary if they had undergone the experiences that had made both Moody and Drummond true believers. Coming from different backgrounds, each man had felt God's love as a transforming experience and wanted to pass it on to others: Moody through his revivals, Drummond through his writing. What they had found was well beyond the powers of mere reason, which both saw as important but also limited in its ability to redeem human lives.

Moody inspired a Yale student named Robert Speer, who went on to produce a 1902 book titled *The Principles of Jesus*. This was the source of the Four Absolutes of the Oxford Group: Love, Purity, Honesty, and Unselfishness. With changes and additions, these evolved over time into a major part of the AA program.

The conflict between science and religion still simmers, but it is slowly being put to rest. We believe today that science can discover nothing that doesn't come from God. There's also agreement that God is Love, and that if He didn't exist, neither could we. And as we move more deeply into a conscious contact with God as Love, we can also let God's Law work in our behalf. This turns out to be nothing more than placing our thoughts and feelings into line with God's will for us, as perceived through prayer and meditation. If we are praying and meditating in the right spirit, our actions will follow the easy-to-understand guidelines laid down by St. Paul in his great definition of Love.

It's hard to believe that two simple books—both easily read in less than two hours—can transform one's life. The hard part is in the practice, which can only occur a day at a time. But when we can understand God as the Law and Love of our lives, we can learn to live—really live, for what might be the very first time. We are the children of God, and therefore we think, we feel, we act, and we love. It's all that simple.

Part Three
The St. Francis Prayer

An Instrument of Peace

by Mel B.

THE INSPIRATION OF ST. FRANCIS

St. Francis of Assisi seems an unlikely person to have made a contribution to AA. That contribution is his famous prayer, which appears in *Twelve Steps and Twelve Traditions* and is now read by AA members around the world. St. Francis is not mentioned by name in the Twelve and Twelve, and is only described as a man who has been rated as a saint for several hundred years. In noting this saintly source, Bill W. went on to say, "We won't be biased or scared off by that fact, because although [St. Francis] was not an alcoholic he did, like us, go through the emotional wringer. And as he came out the other side of that painful experience, this prayer was his expression of what he could then see, feel, and wish to become."

The prayer is known everywhere, and probably came to you last Christmas on a greeting card. Here is how it appears in the Twelve and Twelve:

The St. Francis Prayer

Lord, make me a channel of thy peace—
That where there is hatred, I may bring love—
That where there is wrong,
I may bring the spirit of forgiveness—
That where there is discord, I may bring harmony—
That where there is error, I may bring truth—
That where there is doubt, I may bring faith—
That where there is despair, I may bring hope—
That where there are shadows, I may bring light—
That where there is sadness, I may bring joy.

Lord, grant that I may seek rather to comfort
than to be comforted—
To understand, than to be understood—
To love than to be loved.

For it is by self-forgetting that one finds.
It is by forgiving that one is forgiven.
It is by dying that one awakens to Eternal Life.

Amen.

How did this classic prayer find its way into *Twelve Steps and Twelve Traditions*, which was first published in 1952? In those years, the link to St. Francis was still a link to Catholicism, and Bill W. usually exercised care not to connect AA to any specific religion.

The most likely explanation is that Bill had been given the prayer either by Father Edward Dowling, his close confidante, or perhaps as a result of lessons he had been receiving from Monsignor Fulton J. Sheen, a Catholic priest who had been instrumental in the conversions of several prominent people. However Bill received it, he had been using the prayer as a means of dealing with his own mental depression, which had plagued him from 1944 until about 1956. Writing about his ordeal in the January 1958 *Grapevine*, Bill had said, "I asked myself, 'Why can't the Twelve Steps work to release me from this unbearable depression?' By the hour, I stared at the St. Francis Prayer: 'It is better to comfort than to be comforted.'"

In that same article, Bill stated that he had always been dependent on people and circumstances to supply him with prestige, security, and confidence. Failure to get them had resulted in depression. So he had exerted every ounce of will and action to cut off these unhealthy emotional dependencies. "Then only could I be free to love as Francis had loved," he concluded.

While St. Francis is universally acclaimed as a true apostle of peace, there is one slight problem with the famous prayer attributed to him. There is apparently no way of authenticating him as the prayer's real author, and there's also no record that it appeared before 1915. Almost everyone would agree, however, that the famous prayer captures the thought, philosophy and intention of St. Francis, and that is why it can be so important for the recovering person. Our need is for Peace and Serenity, and Francis found this state of mind and gave it to the world by example.

Since nearly eight centuries have passed since Francis' death in 1226 A.D., some facts about his life may have been altered by legend and myth. But enough is known to assure us that the spirit of the famous prayer attributed to him is a true representation of his approach to life. We also have the Franciscan Order of the Roman Catholic Church as evidence of the traditions he launched in his time. The essence of his life is that he gave up a luxurious lifestyle as the son of a merchant to live in poverty and humility, seeking as much as possible to follow in the footsteps of Christ. There are many reports of the ways he inspired others, and thousands joined his movement, which won the approval of Pope Innocent III.

Though a soldier as a young man, Francis renounced violence and forbade his followers to carry or use weapons. Yet he accompanied the Crusaders to the Holy Land in 1219 and, at the siege of Damietta, even walked through the battle lines to meet the Sultan of Egypt. The Sultan was so impressed by Francis' views on brotherly love that he permitted him to continue his journey to the Holy Land. He later returned to Italy to settle disputes that had arisen among his followers, and also to develop new rules to guide their work. He died in 1226 and was canonized as a saint two years later.

How would Francis respond to the violence and other troubles that confront us today? Based on what we know of his life and work, we can believe that his answer is contained in his famous prayer, and it all begins with a burning desire to know God and to become "an instrument of peace." And while AA members are not in the business of reforming societies and nations, each recovering alcoholic has had to make peace with hordes of personal demons. That makes the famous Peace Prayer especially relevant for our times of stress and conflict.

Notes

[1] *Alcoholics Anonymous*, 3rd ed. (New York: Alcoholics Anonymous World Services, 1976), p. 62.

[2] Bill W., "Why Alcoholics Anonymous Is Anonymous," *Grapevine*, January 1955, reprinted in *The Language of the Heart: Bill W.'s Grapevine Writings* (New York: The AA Grapevine, 1988), pp. 209-218.

[3] *Alcoholics Anonymous*, p. 43.

[4] *Alcoholics Anonymous Comes of Age*, 1st ed. (New York: Alcoholics Anonymous World Services, 1957), p. 39.

About the Author

Mel B. is an AA old-timer, a recovering alcoholic who got sober in Alcoholics Anonymous in 1950 during the early days of the fellowship, while he was a patient in the state hospital in his hometown, Norfolk, Nebraska. He has been an active member of AA for fifty-four years. He is regarded as one of the top historians writing about AA; in addition to this present volume, he has published five other widely read books on the Alcoholics Anonymous program.

New Wine: The Spiritual Roots of the Twelve Step Miracle, 1991
Walk in Dry Places, 1996
Ebby: The Man Who Sponsored Bill W., 1998
The 7 Key Principles of Successful Recovery, 1999 (with Bill P.)
My Search for Bill W., 2000

He was also a contributing writer for *Pass It On*, AA's authorized biography of co-founder Bill Wilson, and has contributed more than fifty articles to the *Grapevine*, the international journal of AA, as well as authoring several Hazelden Foundation pamphlets. Although he discusses topics related to Alcoholics Anonymous in this present volume, the ideas and comments are his own, and he cannot and does not speak for AA as a whole.

He and his wife, Lori, were married in 1960 and have four adult children and eight grandchildren. A resident of Toledo, Ohio, since 1972, he served in public relations for a major corporation headquartered in Toledo until his retirement in 1986. In addition to his AA writings, he has also written publicity material and speeches, and articles on timely business topics and military history.

For more about Mel and his work, see his new website on the internet at www.walkindryplaces.com as well as the AA historical materials on the Hindsfoot Foundation website at www.hindsfoot.org.

0-595-32631-5

Printed in Great Britain
by Amazon